KU-609-459

Kensington and Chelsea Libraries

3 0116 02117855 1

the
BEAUTY
of
IMPOSSIBLE
THINGS

Rachel Donohue graduated from University College, Dublin, in Philosophy and Politics before embarking on a career in communications and media relations. She lives in Dublin. Her debut novel, *The Temple House Vanishing*, was an *Irish Times* bestseller.

the
BEAUTY
of
IMPOSSIBLE
THINGS

RACHEL DONOHUE

CORVUS

Published in Great Britain in 2021 by Corvus, an imprint
of Atlantic Books Ltd.

Copyright © Rachel Donohue, 2021

The moral right of Rachel Donohue to be identified as the
author of this work has been asserted by her in accordance
with the Copyright, Designs and Patents Act of 1988.

All rights reserved. No part of this publication may be
reproduced, stored in a retrieval system, or transmitted
in any form or by any means, electronic, mechanical,
photocopying, recording, or otherwise, without the prior
permission of both the copyright owner and the above
publisher of this book.

This novel is entirely a work of fiction. The names,
characters and incidents portrayed in it are the work of the
author's imagination. Any resemblance to actual persons,
living or dead, events or localities, is entirely coincidental.

10 9 8 7 6 5 4 3 2 1

A CIP catalogue record for this book is available
from the British Library.

Hardback ISBN: 978 1 83895 214 3
Trade paperback ISBN: 978 1 78649 941 7
E-book ISBN: 978 1 78649 943 1

Printed and bound by CPI Group UK Ltd, Croydon CR0 4YY

Corvus
An imprint of Atlantic Books Ltd
Ormond House
26–27 Boswell Street
London
WC1N 3JZ

www.corvus-books.co.uk

MIX
Paper from
responsible sources
FSC® C020471

For S & G, with love.

Champing his gilded oats, the Hippogriff will stand in our stalls, and over our heads will float the Blue Bird singing of beautiful and impossible things, of things that are lovely and that never happen, of things that are not and that should be.

Oscar Wilde, *The Decay of Lying*

Chapter One

I turned fifteen that summer which I never believed to be significant, though afterwards people claimed quite vehemently that it was. I was described as unfinished and open to powers from beyond – a dark ingénue. It is the kind of thing people like to write about young women, as if we were half witch. I should have found it insulting but in all honesty there was too much else to regret. I learned eventually to let their words go, along with much else that was whispered about me. Forgetting became an essential part of getting older and in this way I was exactly like my mother – one of the few traits we ever shared was the ability to avert our gaze from what had gone before. We understood very little, but stayed curious, which was something I suppose.

It is this forgetting which has led my therapist to advise that I return to that lost summer of thirty years ago. She is a very calm lady who I meet every few weeks in a small flat above a bookshop. She speaks about my endeavours to remember in the probing language of closure, encouraging me to retrieve my story and understand better who I once was. This requires some level of optimism and indeed strength of will and I fear I may have lost both along the way, although I don't say this to her as I have tried over time to become more accommodating to the opinions of others. She seems hopeful, which reminds me of my mother sometimes, a blind willingness to want better things for me. I would like not to disappoint her faith. I am reluctant only because it will be a lonely journey, for almost everyone who was there that summer is gone now, and I am quite alone with my thoughts on all that occurred.

When I think back my memories are bleached white, blinded out, as if the sun has erased parts of us. I have glimpses of my mother, distracted and evasive, her brown arm stretched along the back of a deck chair. There would be a glass of something cold in her hands, often wine, that every now and then she would put to her cheek, her sweat leaving a moist stain on the glass. And Mr Bowen, our lodger, his tanned, lean back descending the cliff steps to the beach every morning, a red towel over his shoulders. I see Lewis, always cycling away from me to the Ridge, the large hill that towered over the end of the promenade; his unseasonable black coat blowing in the breeze behind him. Marcus, of course, with his thick blond hair covering those alert, staring eyes and Dr Black too, his cream panama hat tilted at a jaunty angle, impervious to the heat and not a bead of sweat on his elegant brow.

The Beauty of Impossible Things

There was a heatwave that July, this is most definitely fact. It remains the exceptional month to which all the others are compared – we are only ever warmer or colder than that summer. Our small seaside town was heaving with tourists and day trippers. They jostled past each other, eating ice cream or drinking cold beer; their legs splayed as they sat on the side of the promenade, heads turned up to the sky, hoping for a tan; the smell of vinegar on the faint breeze. The sirens of the amusements would be exploding like guns every few minutes to the shrieks of children and at night there were small gorse fires on the Ridge, little spirals of blue smoke marking the evening sky.

It was a strange summer, even before it became tragic. The heat first of all, then the red sand that blew over the ocean from a far-off desert one June morning and dusted the garden. People worried that we were going to get a disease from breathing in its alien particles, with some even suspecting it was a Russian plot, though what that plot might have entailed was never elaborated on. And there were dead flies everywhere, you'd find clumps of them in corners of the room or along the windowsill in the mornings; people mostly blamed the red sand.

The liquid mercury never fell, the afternoons slow and sultry, the heat like a sedative, sucking the oxygen away and slowing your movements. Every step became a commitment you had to think seriously about, a negotiation with invisible forces that pressed against your body and demanded submission. Most nights were too hot for rest and when sleep did finally come, I had anxious dreams about death and the end of the world.

Our old cream-coloured house stood aloof on the cliffs above the town, decrepit and sinking into a lethargy of simmering heat and late-afternoon silence as the summer wore on. The long sash windows staring dolefully out to the sea. A bottle of white wine would be stashed in a bucket of melting ice on the front steps, a blanket unfurled on the grass and a library book upturned and forgotten in the sun. My mother was painting again, so there would be an easel at the edge of the orchard, jars of coloured water at her feet and an unfinished, lonely canvas left aside to dry. She never seemed happy with what she painted and would retreat into the shade with a glass of wine, a large sun hat hiding her eyes, only occasionally throwing furtive glances at her work. She was thirty-three that summer, young really. She had studied art for a few months but never completed her degree, my birth a sort of fatal interruption, so painting was both an escape and a reminder of deep and lasting failure. There was always a brittle pain in her straight back as she stood before the white canvas.

I sometimes think we were made for doing little and completing nothing, and the heat brought out the worst in us both. There was an indolence at the heart of our very being which we always tried to hide, but never quite did. People said it was because we were creative, bohemian even, but I think we were mostly just idle. We were the products of money but the money had all gone, leaving us marooned in a fading dreamland of what once had been. We were an echo and barely real at all, the recipients of both a respect and a dislike that we didn't really deserve. The guests we took in every summer in order to survive were an inconvenience and an embarrassment; we failed them mostly, as we did each other.

Elizabeth, my mother, was probably at her most beautiful. I have come to understand that her face was one of the central, defining features of both our lives and that beauty is far from the superficial thing people like to suggest. It should really be studied more completely, and not by fashion magazines, but by psychologists. Men watched her endlessly, and I spent my life watching them. It became one of my habits. That year her hair was still black and very long, her skin brown with the sun and her eyes large and green, with thick dark lashes. We had Spanish blood and it came out most fully in her, a Mediterranean flavour to her being that she emphasized with colourful scarves and by drinking wine in the middle of the day.

She read books by French authors and talked to me about Marx. She thought exams were an anachronism and never bothered to turn up for parent–teacher meetings or school concerts, but she could be charming if she decided to be, so most people in authority of one kind or another forgave her. And of course she was very beautiful, it disarmed people, interrupted them. People lose themselves in beauty, they lie when they say otherwise.

My mother meanwhile cultivated the idea of freedom, believed that you could and indeed should live a life that did not impinge on others, which was ironic considering her beauty and the way it drew attention to us. She thought it was noble to need almost nothing, to turn your back on convention and be self-sufficient. Despite evidence to the contrary, my birth in particular, she had a sort of puritan's soul. She imagined there was a grandeur and defiance in splendid isolation, in being apart from others. In practice this meant we grew fruit and would spend most of every September soaking, boiling and pouring congealed substances into jars before storing them in a dark cupboard. The house would be filled with the smell of plums, apples, cherries, and to this day the aroma of a stewed apple makes me think not of a pleasurable dessert, but of deprivation and the coming of a long winter.

We bought second-hand clothes and books, had a twenty-year-old car and travelled almost nowhere, though many an evening was spent talking of the places we were going to visit. She took me on a tour of the world from the faded couch in our sitting room, an atlas laid out on the floor, along with ageing travel guides. I was at least twelve before I realized we were never actually going to go anywhere, indeed that she had never been anywhere either. It was all a sort of elaborate dream.

She dressed our way of living up as a philosophy – even as a very small child I remember her talking to me about authenticity and freedom – but in truth much of who we were was driven by poverty and a profound sense of failure, shame even. Our existence was the opposite of freedom, we had few means and could do nothing. We were just eccentric and alone, with little money and ever subject to the scrutiny of those who belonged more easily.

My mother was not vain – I feel I should emphasize this – she held her face at arm's length, like it was a terrible experiment in a jar that had to be kept under wraps for it could explode at any time. She never knew what to do with her beauty really, it was an inheritance that, like our house, was unearned and she felt she had to make up for her good fortune by not wearing make-up and reading about starving people in far-off countries. My birth was part of that in a way, a radical act of deflection, or even self-destruction. She had stepped outside polite society and could never return after my arrival. I too became part of her alternative philosophy for living, both reason and excuse.

It's important to add that I did not look like her. My therapist explains, in kind tones, that perhaps I had a misconception about my external value and it was this that made me feel lesser, an awareness that propelled me to all kinds of strange actions. I try not to laugh when she speaks so, for you only needed a mirror to understand. Beauty is undeniable, one of the many systems of merit at play in a life. I accepted this early on and was never jealous of my mother. I thought she was wonderful, her beauty a kind of statement of intent. I just knew to have been born without a similar face was a particular kind of failing as a woman, as was not having a father, or indeed any money. My shields as a girl in the world were weak from the beginning, and so I had to find other ways to protect myself and find meaning.

It was this understanding of my precarious position that cracked open the summer I turned fifteen, and brought the sky down with it.

Chapter Two

I should explain that my name is Natasha and when I was small a fortune teller in a striped tent on the beach told my mother that I had the mark of the psychic cross on my palm. The woman had large black eyes and many gold rings on her fingers that she tapped rhythmically on the makeshift table between us. She stared at me closely as she spoke and when we got up to leave, she bowed her head.

That night a storm below up along the coast and I woke to my mother singing lullabies beside me in the bed. I explained to her that the fortune teller had come to me in a dream and told me that I had been born before and that to live once was not so special, you needed to do it a few times. As the wind swirled around our house that night, my mother laid her head on the pillow and started to cry, her tears a very clear warning to me – I should speak little about who I really was.

So it became an unspoken vow between us that I remember breaking only once. I was ten and helping her rake up the leaves in the garden one breezy October afternoon, the sun pale and weak, the air biting, the grass slippery and damp underfoot. The rake tangled in the thick weeds and wet earth.

As she worked beside me I stopped to watch the fishermen from the town head out for the afternoon in their small, white trawler, rounding the rocks that edged the foot of the Ridge.

'They won't be coming back,' I whispered to the air.

I could see cold, clear water swirling at their feet, filling the boat, getting higher and higher; could sense the weight of it, dragging them down and under into the endless deep. I heard them shouting and felt their desperate panic. I stayed fixated on the boat, trance-like, as it sailed past the rocks and out of sight, reaching my hands out to the coast. If I was a giant I could have just bent down and plucked them out of the sea, leaving them to rest back on the shoreline.

My mother stopped her work at my words and followed my gaze. Her hand was at her neck, her cheeks flushed, a look of confusion briefly flitted across her features. She knew I was afraid of water and refused to learn to swim. A faltering smile returned then as she tried to reassure me that all would be well.

'They will be home later,' she said, gathering the yellowing, brown foliage.

'No, they won't,' I said, turning to her.

My eyes filled with tears and my hands started shaking uncontrollably. She had to take me into the house and make me hot cocoa. I stayed there alone in front of the fire and watched the afternoon darken into evening, until the first of the flares went up and she came in from the damp garden, her eyes wide with alarm. They didn't come back. They were, all of them, lost at sea – the fathers of my friends Marcus and Lewis among them. The town mourned for months, and some said that none of us ever got over it, my mother included, for she never quite looked at me in the same way again. While I understood that I had failed in the most profound of ways; I might have saved even one life, and did not.

She valued silence. I try and explain this now and it is difficult without making her seem cold, or disinterested. But it was her sacred inner space, and the understanding of my dreams, visions, premonitions – whatever you care to call them – she placed carefully in this silence, along with her own precious but futile desires. I think perhaps she thought if she didn't understand, it might just not be true. She could wish it away.

My therapist suggests I hold buried anger at her conscious ignoring of the very thing that I believe made me special, but I disagree. I understood she had packed the knowledge of my gifts away along with all the other fragile, precious things that were important to her but she could no longer look at. She hid things away, we both did, it was one of the few activities at which we excelled.

I forgive her this.

* * *

The only other person who knew about my psychic abilities was Marcus, my one friend. I don't really know why I had no other friends, or certainly never kept them, but there were no party invitations on our mantelpiece. I didn't dwell on it then, but perhaps I should have. I asked my mother once, many years later, why we never baked cakes or had people over to play for the afternoon. She looked alarmed at the idea and didn't respond. Did I make her strange or did she make me so? It was never very clear.

Marcus lived with his mother in the flat above their fish-and-chip shop on the seafront. In summer they also sold sticks of peppermint rock and hired a candyfloss machine to feed the tourists who had an insatiable appetite for sugar. Marcus had thick, tangled fair hair that half-covered his pale blue eyes and he would stare at you quite meaningfully through the strands. We went to different schools but met at recorder lessons. One day when the music teacher left the room, Marcus hid behind the couch and put me in a tight and painful headlock. He got into trouble for it, even though it was a joke, and he was asked to leave.

Afterwards I used to see him in the window of his shop when I passed by on my way to the lessons – sometimes he would wave and his eyes would be sad. I had a sense even then that there was a long story playing out between us, something deeper and far more unusual than friendship, or even love.

There was a small memorial to Marcus and Lewis's fathers and the other fishermen near the ornate Victorian bandstand on the seafront. If you'd asked me then did we talk about our missing fathers, I would have said no, though now I understand it played a far bigger role in our friendship than we ever admitted. It was like a submerged rock, lying in wait under the water, and we invariably cut ourselves against it every time deep water beckoned.

My father had left for France soon after my birth and moved to a small town on an island off the south-west of the country where he painted for a time, before becoming by all accounts an amusing and popular alcoholic. My mother spoke of him wistfully which is strange when you consider it really, and I always knew a part of her completely understood why he had run away and so forgave him. For a time this worried me greatly. I would trail her around the house and garden, checking she was always in sight, just in case the lure of the sun and my father took her away.

He wrote occasionally and once, when my grandparents were still alive and I was quite little, he invited us to visit. I remembered raised voices in the kitchen. It would have been a step too far to go to him then and perhaps it was easier to forgive from a distance. And so he became another of the ghosts in my life – the most interesting fact about him was his absence, and that he could read palms, something my mother mentioned casually one day.

Marcus said to me once that it was easier having a father who was dead, than one who was missing. He was trying to be nice, but I wasn't sure he was correct, and it wasn't a competition. There were a myriad of ways to be abandoned and each had its own particular way of branding your skin. Lewis, Marcus and I all carried scars – it was what brought us together. I am sure of that now.

When we turned twelve, one wet afternoon in my bedroom I confided in him about my dreams and visions. I had to tell someone and I trusted Marcus completely. We were sitting in front of the small fireplace in my room, the flames spitting as the afternoon darkened outside. When I spoke his eyes became round and his mouth hung open, making him look vaguely stupid. He asked a million questions at first, looking for examples of things I had predicted, then laughed out loud for a bit with joy as if we had discovered the cure for cancer or something important, before finally going quiet and taking my hand. We sat in silence for ages, the only sound the rain blown hard off the coast and the crackle of the fire in the grate. He looked at me differently after that, like I was both invincible and fragile, which I suppose I was in a way.

'What does it feel like?' he would ask endlessly.

'Like you are dissolving,' I would answer.

And it did, it was as if the edges of my being and consciousness faded off into something far bigger than me. Unconstrained by the limits of myself I became part of everyone and everything. I was like liquid seeping into the minds of others, flowing through their thoughts and understanding all they were, and all they tried to hide. I recognize this sounds incredibly odd, but that's how it seemed.

'Does it scare you?' he asked once as we walked on the Ridge.

The sea mist was rolling in off the cliffs, the sodden path winding through the trees ahead, the air all around us vaporous and murky.

'No, never,' I answered.

And he turned back to me and smiled, proud somehow. 'Some day you will do amazing things,' he said.

It was always a gift, you see, though a melancholic one. There was a dark beauty to it, a sense of being connected to the unseen forces that shape our existence. I was privileged really, I knew from very early that our lives were small and built on fragile hope. You could do your best but much was beyond your control, determined elsewhere. I was also quite profoundly naive, and in this way I was, indeed remain, a very ordinary person.

It was how I used my knowledge of the future that I regret. I could have done something different with it, like my mother and her beautiful face.

JUNE

Chapter Three

The story of that long ago summer truly began in the middle of June, on the evening of my fifteenth birthday. Marcus had polished some coloured stones from the beach and along with a box of chocolates and a mix tape wrapped them up and left them on the doorstep. I knew his mother had been involved in the present, certainly the purchase of the chocolates and the wrapping paper. She liked us and would often ask us over for a coffee morning. My mother generally found ways not to go and sometimes I worried that it was because she thought they were slightly beneath us, though she avoided a lot of well-off people too.

That birthday evening, my mother had bought us a takeaway treat which we ate in the garden, listening to the sounds of the seafront far below. She had also got me a bike from a shop in the city, a blue-and-white racer that sparkled in the evening sun. It was the first new bike I had ever owned and she must have saved up for months. We both looked at it leaning against the gate as we ate the sticky, greasy food. It seemed to signify a new stage of independence and intent.

It was close to nine when we finished eating and I decided to take the bike out, dragging it down the narrow cliff steps and on to the seafront which was still relatively quiet, the real summer season still a week or two away. I cycled fast along the promenade, the evening warm, barely a breeze. The bike glided; it had several gears, all of which I tested out, and soft, cushiony handles. It felt almost like flying. I stopped at Marcus's shop to show it off through the glass. He was working behind the counter, doling out onion rings in a white cap. He looked red-faced and I knew he didn't like me seeing him working there, but he seemed impressed.

Continuing along the promenade, waving to the rowers who carried their boat on their shoulders down to the shoreline, I cycled to the edge of the Ridge. Marcus knew to find me there when his shift finished close to ten p.m. Locking the bike carefully to the last of the street lights near the small train station, I walked in the low pink sun through the sandy scrub grass and up the hill to the edge of the trees. I never liked to go too much further into the woods on my own. It was a desolate place, lonely, with dense firs and narrow cliff paths that led to secluded clearings which were guarded by large, moss-covered boulders where people would light fires and smoke drugs. A few people had even killed themselves up there and I always imagined I could sense their lost spirits hidden amongst the trees, ever watchful. Couples went too in the evenings, their cars parked up on the sand.

I sat in the grass for almost an hour as the town began to light up below. Music drifted from the bars, the deep bass line throb of 'Stairway to Heaven' trapped in the still, warm air. I could see my house in the distance, windows alight and staring out to sea in its lonely manner. It was a transient, once-elegant town, with tall, decaying pastel-coloured houses along the seafront, truly alive for only a few months of the year. It was near enough to the city to be aware of all that it was missing, and not far enough away to be considered particularly interesting. I think now that all of us who lived there had a native inferiority complex, a sense that we were not quite good enough. We belonged to a place of leisure and forgetting, mere snapshots of people. I loved it though, in my own way.

That night I thought about turning fifteen, how it seemed quite a significant age, and I wondered vaguely what it was I was supposed to do with my life. My father drifted into my head then, a fleeting idea of a man, and I wondered what, if anything, he might expect of me. There was one of his paintings in the attic, lurid thick colours, that had been laid on with a knife, pulsating from the canvas. As a small child I had taken to pressing my face right up close to it and tracing the movement of the paint across the surface, gorges and cliffs of rough colour. I imagined him Picasso-like, stripped to the waist, with a blade in his hand.

As the hour passed, I missed Marcus, glanced at my watch and wondered briefly why he hadn't come. I worried about him sometimes, he had been in fights with some boys from his school at the end of term. There was a restlessness in him, a boredom which I felt in myself too, as if all the things that summer had once meant to us no longer seemed true or very interesting. We were pressing hard against the limits of something we had not yet been able to define.

As the light dwindled I got up to head home and gazed back up the Ridge. It was forbidding as ever, brown-, purple- and gold-coloured in the fading light. It had always seemed too large for the town below, like an accident of nature, the only large hill for miles and we seemed to crouch beneath it. I closed my eyes for a second and breathed in the smell of coconut from the gorse and the earth, an odour distinctive to the Ridge. There was the sharp crack of a bird's wing far above me and I imagined it soaring high into the empty space of the night. I envied its wild freedom and opened my eyes.

This was when I first saw them.

The trees were starkly outlined against the orange of the sky and deep within the woods small, blue lights were flickering and sparking in the gloom. They swooped and turned between the black of the heavy, entwined branches as if they were doing silent somersaults, turning and rolling, rising to the treetops, then falling sharply. It was enthralling, like a secret fireworks show, and I briefly stepped forward from the sandy path to the edge of the burned grass that marked the beginning of the forest. I reached my hand out as if drawn in by some magic and I could feel my own breaths rise and fall with them; there was a rhythm to the movement they made that seemed not outside of me any more, but deep within. The air was cracking around me with a harsh energy; the lights began to move faster then, darting among the trees, moving in circles, ever quicker, dizzying, and I felt nauseous and needed to look away, but before I could they soared suddenly again to the top of the dark trees, disappearing into the sky. I strained my eyes, trying to see where they had gone, my neck tilted back, but they had disappeared. It must have lasted less than a minute and I felt numb, paralyzed almost, standing there in the twilight while the air all around me seemed to reverberate and shimmer with both threat and possibility.

They left as quickly as they had come and I stayed staring upwards for a few seconds longer, both willing them to return and afraid that they actually might. I felt winded, as if I had run a race, and my stomach had butterflies. I bent over and took some deep breaths to steady myself. The breeze picked up suddenly then and the trees began to creak; an eerie, painful sound as if they were starting to come alive, their limbs cracking as they awoke from an eternal slumber. It would be dark soon.

I ran down the sandy path of the Ridge in fear, unlocking my bike and cycling home quickly, too afraid to look at the sky above me. The journey back seemed to take for ever, the distance stretched out and the sights strangely unfamiliar; the promenade empty and desolate, rubbish blowing across my path. The lights were out in Marcus's takeaway, they had shut early. For a moment I believed I was the only one left in the town and everyone had been vanished away, but then as I sped past the bandstand I saw Lewis, a lonely shadow, standing in the centre of the empty stage. My bike screeched and stuttered to a halt, coming to rest in front of the wilting flowers that lay on the stone memorial for his and Marcus's fathers. A handwritten prayer covered in plastic was attached to the stone, fluttering in the breeze.

Lewis lived in the cottages on the far side of the town and was nineteen that summer. He was not well, though no one ever really explained what was wrong with him. My mother said he had suffered a nervous breakdown but even this didn't shed much light on the matter. I knew when he was younger his teacher had thought he was going to be a genius but around the time of his thirteenth birthday he had been found speaking some kind of broken gibberish in the middle of a roundabout outside the town, picking wildflowers as the cars went past. He'd been in a hospital for a while after that incident and given medication to take. It's to balance him, my mother had explained, to keep his moods in check. She always looked sad when she said this. He was a favourite of hers; some evenings he would climb the cliff steps to our house and sit in the garden and she would give him our home-made lemonade.

Lewis walked slowly to the locked, small gate at the top of the steps of the bandstand and looked down at me, his face pale and shining in the anxious yellow glare of the street lamps.

'Lights.' He pointed to the sky above the Ridge.

He had seen them also and for a brief second I wanted to cry with relief, and hold him. A man let out a deep, savage scream somewhere in the back end of the town, and there was the sound of glass shattering, followed by raised voices. Lewis looked past me to the promenade for a second, before holding his thin hands out to me and moving his fingers up and down to mimic something flashing.

'Like spirits,' he whispered.

'I know, I know.' I was too unnerved to look back in its direction.

I had such a strong desire to dump my bike and hold him close, but he didn't like that – outside of his family my mother was the only one he ever permitted to touch him.

'They have come back,' he said.

I wondered if he had seen the lights before and what it was he knew about them. The noises in the back street of the town grew louder, a fight was breaking out which was not unusual on those nights.

'I have to go home, you do too, go home now. . . we'll talk about it again, OK?' I said, pointing furiously in the direction of his house.

He nodded sadly at me but didn't move and I could feel his eyes on my back as I cycled home.

I slept little that night.

* * *

Marcus was the only person I told about the sighting the next day. He looked shocked, enthralled and then a little bit afraid – unexplained lights on the Ridge, what could it mean? He very much regretted not coming to meet me and was envious of Lewis for having witnessed it too, but he had been made to clean the storeroom that night.

We talked about what I had seen often in the days afterwards and spent a few long afternoons huddled over books about 'extraterrestrial encounters' and 'ghost lights' in the library. We were keeping all options open but the supernatural of some kind or other seemed like a logical conclusion, to me anyway.

'Aliens?' he said, eyebrows raised.

'Maybe ghosts? The people who killed themselves up there,' I replied.

The librarian tutted and put her finger to her lips. I tried to explain to him how it had felt, as if the air was cracking, in some way sparking, and that the trees were whispering and the lights were like little souls, floating. They were trying to tell me something. Marcus looked perplexed.

'People go there especially to die,' I said.

The Ridge, a lonely graveyard of restless souls.

In the nights that followed my sighting I had a series of strange, intense dreams in which I was flying high above the Ridge, bathed in blue light, with wild, roaring, angry water beneath me. Lewis was in them and Marcus too, both of them crying or separated from me by water; my hands would reach out to try and grip them but they always slipped away. My mother featured in one too, she was collecting apples in the orchard but the trees kept dissolving into water every time she touched them. I woke gasping for air in the dead, dark heat of my bedroom.

'Perhaps I'm supposed to warn everyone,' I said to Marcus one afternoon about a week after the sighting, towards the end of June.

The lights had appeared on my birthday, the very night I was trying to understand who I was and what my purpose in life might be. It was perhaps all connected. A mystical message, demanding I accept my fate as a prophet and not hide any more.

'Why do you think something bad is going to happen? It could mean something else,' he said.

'The dreams I've had since, but also that night, it felt

ominous, like heavy, despairing almost, but also strangely beautiful. Like you might want to stay up there, if you were brave enough.'

Marcus kicked some stones and stared at the sea. 'It always smells of death on the Ridge,' he said finally.

Chapter Four

Two things happened then which I have ever since tied together. Mr Bowen, our new lodger, arrived to stay and Marcus shoved a note under the front door. I found the note first which in his scrawled writing stated that we needed to meet urgently as there had been 'news'. I went into the kitchen where my mother was painting her nails at the window and leaving tiny stabs of colour on the sill.

'I'm going to see Marcus,' I said.

She nodded her head in response while blowing gently on her nails and seemed generally unconcerned that the house was a mess and our paying guest was due.

It was already warm in the garden when I went outside. The marmalade cat lay asleep in the weeds that lined the gravel path, and I could hear the far-off jingle of an ice-cream van on the seafront. A lonely call for early-rising children. I walked to the gate that led down the cliff to the promenade, covering my eyes from the glittering glare of the sea, and that's when I saw Mr Bowen for the first time.

He was a tall, straight figure with black hair walking up from the station below, suitcase in hand. He wove his way patiently and carefully along the uneven steps that led up the cliffs from the seafront, stopping halfway to look back at the sea and the few early-morning bathers wading out on the beach below. He must have taken the first train from the city. I waited for him to continue his climb upwards but he didn't move. I made a bet that if he turned and showed me his face he would fall in love with my mother. I did things like that, pretended the universe and I were engaged in an elaborate and complex game of cards. Mr Bowen, however, refused to obey.

He stared out to sea and the strange sky, his back turned away, his light grey shirt rising and falling in the warm breeze – perhaps it wasn't challenge enough, they were all in love with her. I spoke softly to myself then, breathed out the words into the warm air and closed my eyes for a second like it was a prayer:

This time she will fall in love with him.

It all seemed like an amusing distraction, though one I would come to regret.

He turned then and continued his way slowly up the cliff steps. I hid behind the hydrangeas in the garden and waited for him to pass.

* * *

After avoiding Mr Bowen, I ran along the promenade and headed to the bandstand. There was a smell of candyfloss and chips in the air and every now and then an alarm went off down the coast. The trucks with all the amusements were lined up on the road, their sides open and boxes being carried out. They were preparing for a bumper weekend of visitors.

Marcus walked quickly towards me. His red shorts seemed too small, as if he had grown overnight. Every day there seemed to be something different about him – more fine hair on his arms and his face, or his hands seemed to be bigger. He was expanding into the world, taking up more space. I jumped from the steps of the bandstand and with only a glance exchanged, we walked in the direction of the Ridge. The people thinned out around us and the path went from concrete to sandy, reedy grass as we climbed up the steep hill. The sun was hot on our heads and the air felt like it was folding in on itself, becoming more dense as we walked.

'I shaved my hair.' He pushed up his floppy, damp, fair hair to show a razored underside.

I nodded an enthusiastic approval. I could see the outline of his pale skull. We walked on in silence for a minute. We were OK with silence, it never felt uncomfortable, and besides I could understand his thoughts. There were not many of them sometimes, by which I do not mean to suggest that he was not very bright, or an empty person, for he wasn't. I just used to feel like his head had wide-open spaces in it, like prairie fields, and

31

there was meaning in the silence and the expanse. My head was different, jumbled up and cluttered. A shaft of sun hit the sea far off in the bay and the water closer to the cliffs looked a deep green.

We passed a black bike with a basket thrown on the grass. It belonged to Lewis but he was nowhere in sight. He had been away with his mother visiting relatives and I hadn't seen him since the night of the lights almost ten days earlier.

Marcus and I pushed through the scratchy, yellow gorse bushes to the side of the path where there were some large rocks to sit on and you were hidden from view. There was ash and charcoal on the ground where a fire had died out. Marcus sat cross-legged and sucked on a long piece of grass, making a whistling sound. He squinted in the sun, looking at the Ridge looming above us. His skin appeared damp and flushed and he smelled of candyfloss and dried sweat; there was dirt under his nails.

'I've been working out.' He clenched the muscles in his arm in front of my face.

His arm looked impressive, taut and bulging at the same time. He was also wearing a bronze bracelet I had not seen before. I touched it and he took it off and gave it to me.

'My father's,' he explained, head down, looking at the ground.

'It's lovely,' I said, my cheeks flushed, handing it quickly back to him.

I had a deep sense of guilt whenever he mentioned his father, I don't know why really as it was not my loss to own and there was nothing I could have done differently that day in the garden. I just felt I had failed him. It was the same with Lewis.

'Mum said I was old enough to wear it now, and not lose it.'

He laughed then and tilted his head back into the sun.

He was quite beautiful sometimes, everything about him bright and shining; his yellow hair and glistening skin. Today the sunlight was glinting off a can that was discarded and jammed between the rocks – it created a strip of blinding light at his feet and he seemed to shimmer in the heat haze.

'What's the news?' I dug the heels of my runners back and forth into the dusty ground.

'Other people saw the lights,' he said, looking at me through his hair.

'Who?' My voice was suddenly shaky and high-pitched.

'Holiday kids, they were in the shop talking about it last night, they said there were blue shining things in the trees and then they disappeared.' He sounded mildly affronted on my behalf and went back to fiddling with his bracelet.

'When did they see them?' I asked.

'Two nights ago, they were camping on the Ridge,' he replied, reaching down to pick at a scab on his leg.

It was a relief but also disconcerting to think people other than Lewis and I had seen them. I wondered briefly if perhaps the message they brought wasn't meant for me after all, but I pushed that thought away. If anything it meant something big was truly happening, we were being contacted by something not of this world.

'Did they describe them?' I whispered now and leaned towards him slightly.

'They said they were blue, rolling, like what you saw, they called them ghost lights too.' He gestured with his hand.

'Interesting.'

Marcus didn't respond. He was always funny when it came to the tourists. When we were younger we had run a small detective agency and spent several days following some tourists and taking down their car registration numbers. The activities of the tourists interested us quite a bit. In truth they seemed to have better, more exciting lives than us, though we never explicitly admitted that. It would have been hard to take.

'Ghost lights are supposed to try and lead people away, it was in one of those books in the library,' I said.

'You didn't imagine it then,' he said quietly.

His hair covered his eyes and it made me want to brush it away and release his gaze fully. He would say things and then retreat and I found it annoying.

'Of course I didn't, Lewis saw them too, you know that.' I was surprised he had ever doubted. 'Are you afraid?' I asked.

'Why would I be afraid?' He raised his eyebrows like I had insulted him.

'I had another dream last night.' I lowered my voice.

He sat up straighter and stared at me, his eyes serious and locked steadily on mine.

'I was sitting in the garden and the blue lights were in the orchard. Then the sea started to rise, it was getting higher and higher, it was rising up the cliffs and reaching the garden. Then it was night suddenly, the lights were gone and I could see nothing, there was just the sound of water, getting nearer and nearer and a whispering in my ear, voices calling me to come into the water, like they were sirens or something.'

I drifted back to the feeling of it, the heaviness, shadows enveloping me and the air damp as the waters crept ever closer. 'And I sort of wanted to go with them,' I said.

Marcus looked lost and dreamy, enveloped in my words. He had told me once he liked the way I spoke – I put things in an odd order apparently and it made nothing I said seem certain, or ordinary.

'What does it mean?' he asked quietly, his voice deep and serious.

I loved when he asked me questions like that, and perhaps it was about power of a kind, though I don't think so really. It was like being in the sun when he stared at me. If my words made him feel uncertain, his presence had quite the opposite effect on me.

Before I could answer him though there was a sudden, heavy thud behind us on the path and a shout. We both jumped and Marcus looked at me with alarm before putting his finger on his lips and gesturing to me to wait; he pushed gently through the gorse.

'It's Lewis,' he called back to where I was sitting before disappearing into the thicket and onto the path.

I went after him quickly and saw Lewis getting up off the ground and rubbing dust from his clothes. He was wearing the large black suit that must have once belonged to his father. His hair, usually hidden under a tweed cap, was lank and long at the side of his face and he was sweating, his cheeks a furnace red. Marcus walked over to him but as he got near, Lewis, with startled eyes, shoved him away roughly and picked up his bike, pushing it as quickly as he could down the scrub path back to the seafront. It bumped and rattled along the uneven surface.

'Lewis,' I cried after him but he didn't turn.

'He was crying,' said Marcus faintly.

We both watched his narrow back disappear from sight.

'You know he once said to me that he didn't feel different on the inside – he described it like he was divided in two almost. I thought it was sad but really intelligent too, like a part of him is the same as it was before, it's just hard to find, or he keeps losing it,' I said.

Marcus rubbed his head but didn't reply. Lewis made him

uncomfortable and I presumed it was because their dads had died together. People always lumped their names into the one sentence when discussing that day – the lost boys. He didn't want to be like Lewis and he didn't want to be included in the pity.

'Why are you working out?' I asked, shading my eyes and seeking to change the subject.

It seemed unusual, not something he would ever have done before.

'I just want to get strong.' He shrugged his shoulders.

'Barclay's are starting a gym in their yard, in the evenings, I might go,' he finished.

Barclay's was a garage at the back end of the town. Some older kids hung out there in the evenings and there was a rumour that you could get drugs, if you wanted.

'I might not too though,' he said, watching for my reaction.

His words got caught in the light breeze and were flung over the edge to the sea. The sun was searing and sharp on my head and I felt the back of my neck start to burn. There were shouts and clapping down on the seafront, the Big Dipper had been turned on. It wasn't a proper, big roller coaster, but the name stuck and a small crowd had gathered to watch, they always did. I turned away from Marcus and looked up to the Ridge, steep and shadowy behind us.

'What does your dream mean?' he asked again, rubbing the sweat from his forehead.

I covered my eyes from the white heat of the sun.

'It means something is coming, and it will take us over.'

I truly believed that.

Chapter Five

When I got home, I found the dining-room table looking surprisingly tidy and set for our first lunch with Mr Bowen. The blue drapes were pulled back from the French doors and tied neatly. The room, though, felt musty and warm, and the salmon-coloured roses in a bowl in the centre of the table were already wilting. I opened the French doors to the garden to air it out, but there was no breeze outside, just dead afternoon heat.

'Can I help?' he called from the hall.

I presume my mother answered no to his question because he wandered into the dining room then, holding a bottle of wine. He was handsome, with cornflower-blue eyes and very black hair, a freshness to his complexion, as if he had just run a race, or been swimming. I remember in that moment he made me think of woods and ice, like something out of a Nordic tale. He was tall and hunched a little. He put the wine on the table and then offered his hand.

'Natasha, a pleasure,' he said, smiling.

He felt warm and his voice was pleasant, cultured, confident even but his eyes looked unsure and he nervously pulled at his collar. He came from the city and was forty-five years old, he taught English literature in the university. He had written a number of books which, when I look back now, should have made me like him. It was unusual to have an author visit the town.

My mother followed closely behind Mr Bowen with a jug of her consommé soup. She was wearing her faded pink summer dress, with a light silk shawl over it, and had caught her hair up in a low bun. We all stood around the table and smiled awkwardly, a strange formality between us. Mr Bowen sat down opposite me and began to stare at the framed photographs on the wall behind. They were yellowing portraits of long-dead ancestors, children with vacant eyes in tiny sailor suits and a solemn baby in a giant pram.

'They watch over us and mostly disapprove,' said my mother, noticing his gaze and starting to laugh.

She looked young, she was still young and she liked to laugh at things. My therapist reminds me of this sometimes, she wants me to see her as she was, not perhaps how I would have liked her to be. Mr Bowen went faintly red as if he had made some error and looked down at his plate. We began to eat then.

'You must have an excellent archive, family records and photos here, I suppose?' he asked.

I would learn he was a serious person, took things seriously and thought about them in a way we did not. We were careless in comparison. He believed in knowledge, reason, and should really have found us frivolous, but he didn't. He saw the tragedy.

'Well, yes, not in any organized way, but more as custodians.' She flicked her green eyes to me briefly and willed me to say nothing.

I thought of the attic filled with rotting boxes of pictures and half-finished paintings and how we almost never went up there as it was depressing and made you think of death.

'It's lovely, the house, the sea. It is everything I was looking for this summer,' he said.

My mother watched him thoughtfully as we ate, her spoon in mid-air over her bowl. He raised his head to her. They didn't speak but looked at each other for a brief moment. He leaned back in his chair then and nodded at me, smiling, and there was something true about it, hopeful even. He seemed relieved, as if things might have gone far worse. My mother crinkled her forehead briefly before getting up and collecting the bowls off the table.

'Do you swim much?' He wiped his mouth with the napkin.

I shook my head. 'I never learned.'

He raised his eyebrows and then looked out of the French doors into the garden, where butterflies were floating around the honeysuckle.

'I did get lessons but they didn't work. I don't like putting my head underwater or being told what to do really,' I explained.

He turned back and smiled. He had good teeth, all straight and apparently his own.

'It was beautiful today in the water, I felt alive, re-born even,' he said, then laughed as if he had found some kind of magical sanctuary from the world.

The sounds of the seafront could be heard faintly, whoops and cheers, clapping, and in the far distance, the smashing of glass.

'I can give you some lessons one morning, if you like?' He leaned forward in his chair.

He looked at me carefully, sincerely even, and I felt, as I often would that summer, as if he was there to examine our characters. There was something personal in his questioning, a sense of him looking, watching as he tried to understand the world he had stepped into. He assumed nothing about us, which I see now was quite unusual, most people made quick judgements.

'I got a new bike for my birthday, it was two weeks ago,' I said.

'Nice,' he replied.

I thought he might ask me my age, most adults did, but he just took a drink of his wine. My mother returned holding hot plates, a dishcloth protecting her hands because she always left them too long in the oven. She leaned down to place one in front of him but the timing was off and it touched the inside of his wrist. He recoiled at the burn, pushing his chair sharply back from the table as my mother flashed her eyes to me in helpless panic. I wondered if it would scar.

I went quickly to the kitchen and doused a clean cloth with cold water. When I got back to the dining room, she was on her knees beside his chair, holding his arm. I gave her the cloth. She pushed a stray hair behind her ear and leaned closer to him, placing the damp material on his wrist – he shut his eyes briefly in relief, before opening them again to look down at her. Her shawl slipped to the floor and he used his unburned arm to pick it up for her.

We ate for a time in semi-silence after this, the gold carriage clock on the mantelpiece ticked and in the corner the fan whirred more slowly than usual as if the motor was failing. The air felt dead, even though the doors to the garden were still wide open, there was not a breath and I could feel sweat on my neck. My mother looked like a da Vinci painting – shadowy and mysterious. He dabbed the corner of his mouth a bit too often and when he took a drink I noticed he watched her intently over the glass.

'You have lovely books in your study, first editions,' he said, nodding.

'My grandfather was a collector.' Her tone was dismissive, the words flung on the table.

He watched her speak and a faint smile played on his lips,

as if her reply was something he already knew, or had expected.

'I'd like to collect, but it's too expensive.'

'You teach English?' I asked and he nodded.

'I don't read old books really, the sentences are so dense, they put me off. I feel like they are punishing me for not completing my education,' my mother added.

'You've read Tolstoy,' I said.

I was always protective of her, the curse of the child who was more aware of the opinions of others than their parent. You lived a hyper-aware existence, conscious of the slights they didn't see, a surplus of empathy that eventually stagnated into something else.

'He's different,' she replied, looking down.

Mr Bowen wiped his brow and looked hot, breathless almost.

'And Chekov,' I said.

She threw me a pained glance.

'I like *The Great Gatsby*,' I said.

'That's a novella,' my mother replied.

'I know.'

Mr Bowen took a long drink. He seemed like a man with an endless, desperate thirst. My mother stared out of the window, a determined look to her profile, as if she was preparing for a battle of some sort. Her moods rose and fell quickly, you got used to it.

'It's a good book,' said Mr Bowen.

'I never liked Daisy.' She stared into the greenery.

'No, she is unappealing.'

I wondered would he be able to follow her thoughts, to chase them down the wandering paths they travelled and not be upended by her curiosity and fleeting mood about things. Most men just talked at her, or stared.

'More people should write novellas, so many books are really too long,' she said.

'Is *Breakfast at Tiffany's* a novella or a short story?' I asked.

Neither of them answered, but stayed staring at each other across the table.

'The actual book, whichever it is anyway, is better than the film.' I looked from one to the other. 'She's really a prostitute you know, that doesn't come across in the film.'

My mother threw her eyes up to heaven briefly.

'I haven't seen the film or read the book,' said Mr Bowen.

'We have an excellent library here, they order things for you too, if they don't have them. Why have you come here to write anyway?' I asked.

My mother sighed loudly and then coughed to cover it up.

'A good question. . .' He looked at me.

He seemed very warm, a dewy glow to his skin, and his neck was flushed red down to the open button of his white shirt. He pulled at it again.

'I needed some quiet time,' he drew in his lips as he spoke.

'What's the book about?' I asked.

'A Russian soldier who deserts the army.'

'But if he deserted, that's not brave, doesn't a hero need to be brave?'

'He had his reasons, I think,' he smiled.

'If more men deserted their causes it would probably be better for the world,' my mother said, taking a drink and then pressing the cold glass to her hot cheek.

He looked at her with a kind of burning, interested wonder.

'Which war?' she asked.

'Napoleonic,' he answered.

'How many words do you write every day?' I asked.

He dragged his gaze from her and back to me.

'It depends, sometimes I disappear for hours, the words just come, other days it is very painful and I feel like a complete failure.'

It was an alarming admission really and I wondered why he felt comfortable speaking so. I was not used to men who ever admitted they failed at anything, even Marcus always attempted to seem like a hero, however small the achievement.

'It takes time to find the way sometimes,' said my mother, her eyes large and haunted.

He looked up at her with thankfulness. I had forgotten that air of gratitude that hung around them. It was there in the house every day after he came, almost as much as the desire, as if luck had descended from on high and brought them together. It was of course the opposite, but they didn't see that.

'You should make it a novella instead.' I wiped my mouth with the napkin.

He laughed then and it was both easy yet masterful, commanding somehow, he was a man in our house and he would move and live differently in the space with us. It would become something other with him there.

'You are painting?' he asked my mother.

'I dabble. . . it's nothing really,' she replied, a flush on her cheeks.

'I'm sure that's not the case.'

'It is,' she responded sharply.

She looked at him with irritation and he flushed red.

I knew when she needed saving in social situations, when people's presumptions about her spilled out and she would either retreat or hit back, so I tried to intervene.

'When I think of Vincent Van Gogh's time in the yellow house, I sometimes want to cry – if only he'd known that his work was great,' I said.

They didn't answer and stayed looking at each other in some kind of a mutually curious yet intense standoff.

'Would your other books be in the library in town?' she asked.

'Possibly.' He looked down at his plate again.

'It's like Henry VIII in England – if only he'd known Elizabeth was going to be an OK queen, he needn't have bothered trying to have a son,' I said.

My mother laughed out loud then, as if it were just the two of us there, and she leaned across the table to touch my cheek. She always said they felt like satin, with no blemishes. She then touched her own cheek. I never knew if she was aware that she did this, a mirroring.

'Honestly, we do have the oddest conversation. I'm not sure everyone would agree Elizabeth I was an "OK queen" – you must excuse us,' she said, looking back to him.

We weren't supposed to talk about history, politics or religion with the guests. Sport was out too, but that was because we didn't know anything about it.

'Pretend I'm not in the room.' He rubbed his forehead.

'Did you hear? There were some strange blue lights in the sky apparently over the Ridge. I heard about it in town today, there was a man talking about them on the television too, an investigator or some such.' She was addressing me.

She started to collect the plates off the table and Mr Bowen looked at me with interest.

'I did hear.' I handed her my plate.

He thanked her for the lunch and said it was delicious. She looked embarrassed and stood up from the table. I could hear a fly buzzing at the threshold of the French doors, deciding whether to enter the hot room or not.

'I saw them too,' I said.

I breathed deeply, aware that I was defying her, breaking my unspoken promise to never speak of the odd things I saw.

'What?' She stopped in the doorway.

'It's a warning that something bad is going to happen,' I replied.

My words were stark, like giant black letters dropped from the ceiling. A knife slipped out of her hand and clattered on the floor. Mr Bowen jumped up from his chair and went to retrieve it, awkwardly trying to lay it back on the now lopsided plates in her grasp. Her face was pale as she stared at me, and Mr Bowen turned briefly too, unsure and out of place.

We could have been a family of sorts, I suppose, if things had been different, but it wasn't to be. He was as lost as the rest of us in the heat of that summer, more so perhaps, for they never found his body.

Chapter Six

The next day an extraordinary article appeared in the local paper giving other witness accounts of the lights and quoting a Dr Black, a paranormal investigator who was on his way to the town. Mr Bowen frowned while reading it in the kitchen, his towel over his shoulder, and then passed the paper to my mother. She glanced at the headline and drank some coffee.

'I'm going for a swim.' He looked awkwardly from one of us to the other.

But we didn't answer.

'And then I'll be working in my room,' he said, escaping into the hall.

I ran into the garden after him. The air was heavy and sweet, the cat was curled up in the lavender and looked up briefly at us before lying down again.

'You don't have to be part of this,' my mother called from the door.

'I already am.' I turned back to look at her.

But she had retreated into the cool darkness of the hallway.

I went looking for Marcus but he wasn't in the takeaway so I headed to the beach where there was a crowd of boys standing in a circle. They were mostly tourists but alarmingly Lewis was in the centre of the group, hopping on the sand, his arms punching into the air. It looked like a strange dance. His black shirt had fallen loose from his baggy trousers and was occasionally riding up and showing his thin belly. I could see Marcus standing in the crowd, his yellow hair always the distinguishing feature. His arms were folded and his face seemed to be in a pose of studied nonchalance.

Sand was flying and Lewis was making his high snarling sound. I wasn't quite sure what was going on until another boy suddenly stepped forward and pushed him easily to the ground, the crowd moved closer. I expected Marcus to try and help, but he stayed on the edge of it, transfixed by the spectacle of it all. I pushed further through the sweaty crowd to get closer. Lewis was pinned to the ground now and the other boy was straddling him, his hand in a fist and threatening to strike. Lewis's thin legs were kicking and straining, there was sand in the air. Some of the boys started chanting, 'Do it, do it. . .'

There was a tight knot in my chest, and my throat was dry but I stepped quickly into the empty circle to a sharp intake of collective breath and grabbed the boy on top of Lewis by the ear. He felt sweaty and fleshy and he slipped off him easily and onto the sand. The boys behind me went silent. As he lay on the ground I kicked him in his side before he could get up; he shielded his head. Lewis jumped up then, offered me a panicked stare, his face red and a thin line of blood on his lips before running away towards the bandstand.

'Don't touch him again,' I shouted to the boy who was curled up now like a baby.

I turned back to the others who were staring at me. Marcus shifted uneasily and looked to the boys either side of him, before glancing back to me.

'Stupid cow,' someone shouted.

Marcus winced and flicked a sullen eye to the boy who had spoken.

'The lights over the Ridge are coming back,' I said, running my eyes over the crowd.

In the distance a train was making its way from the city, inching along the edge of the coast towards our small station. Marcus looked at me open-mouthed and I heard the others whispering under their breath about the story in the paper – only some had heard about the lights. A few looked up towards the Ridge and shifted uneasily when the detail had been explained.

'They will be back, tomorrow night, and it's a warning – something dark and terrible is on its way,' I said.

I don't really know what made me speak so explicitly at that moment except that I felt charged with a desire to explain things, to make them understand and respect me – to see me, even. And in my defence, I knew from my dreams it was not going to be an ordinary summer, something was coming, and it was only right that people knew. Perhaps a part of me wanted to frighten them.

I was once asked many years after by a serious man, with thin gold-rimmed glasses in a fancy office, if I desired notoriety because I had felt so distinctly unimportant. I told him I had just wanted to be myself. I still think that was true. I was in search of my mother's holy grail of authenticity. The only problem was, no one really wanted the real me, it was too disturbing, and my attempts at honesty slipped sadly into fear and ill repute.

Suddenly the amusements roared into life further down the beach, accompanied by sirens and shouts of joy; children stood at the top of the helter-skelter and one by one slipped down the twists and turns, emerging onto the hot sand. The boys started to walk away, some of them throwing glances back as they disappeared down the beach. Marcus was still, watching me, and for a brief second it was as if we had never met before, a stranger in his eyes.

'Are the lights really coming back?' He walked slowly towards me then.

He looked filled with doubt, a frown on his brow, and for some reason there was a catch in my throat and I didn't know quite what to say.

* * *

My mother was nowhere to be found when I got home an hour or so later, but the door of the house was on the latch and the cat was lying in the shade of the porch, so I expected she was nearby. The house felt airless, dust dry, and the stairs creaked and sighed as I went upstairs in search of a book. Mr Bowen's door across from mine was shut tight and there was no sound; he must have been writing.

I heard voices in the garden then and leaned out of my window. My mother and Lewis had climbed the steps up from the seafront together. He was holding her basket, swinging it until she took it from him, and gestured for him to sit. She then took a handkerchief out of her pocket and began dabbing at the cuts on his forehead and cheek. He didn't wince once but kept smiling at her, and every now and then he tried to hold her hand. He saw me at the window then and stood up.

'Your lights are blue.' He pointed excitedly to the Ridge in the distance.

The cat wandered over and brushed against his legs before disappearing into the orchard and my mother reached up, trying to coax him to sit back down with her, but he got agitated and nervous, moving away from her to stand under my window. When I ran out into the garden my mother indicated he had gone into the orchard. I found him sitting in the long grass. He smiled when I sat down beside him. It was cool and shady there, white butterflies and wasps danced around us, the cat wandered past, eyes wide and her tail curled.

'I'll find out what the lights are, I'll understand them and then I'll tell you about it,' I said.

It was a habit, to think you knew more than Lewis did. One of the many small cruelties inflicted on him by people who thought they were trying to be kind.

'I've been to the library and I think it might be ghosts, or ghost lights with a warning of some sort. Lights like these have been seen in many other places around the world, not exactly the same but. . .' I tried to explain.

I reached out to touch his hand but he withdrew it sharply.

'That night on the bandstand, you said they came back. Have you seen them before?' I asked.

He looked up at the sky through the green of the leaves and his face was mottled, light and shade.

'They are always there. In the trees on the Ridge'.

'I don't think so, I've never seen them before, no one has.'

The sun disappeared briefly behind a lone cloud and the orchard was no longer golden but a deep green, as if we were submerged in water.

'I'm going to die,' he whispered, still staring at something above his head. He spoke as if it was the most ordinary of things to say.

'Don't,' I said, reaching out again before remembering and pulling my hand back.

As I said the word his pale, wet face came back to me as it had been in my dream. He was sinking under the water and

I was desperately trying to pull him back from the hungry waves, but he refused to take my hand.

Chapter Seven

The next evening Marcus and I went to meet Mike Ryan, the journalist who wrote the story about the lights; he was sitting in a café opposite the casino wearing sunglasses on the top of his head and smoking a Marlboro red. Every now and then the door of the casino across the street swung open far enough so that you could see the flashing lights and hear the sounds of the slot machines within. It was not a part of the town I was supposed to visit. People gambled from early morning until midnight, they always looked exhausted and poorly fed, as if they had forgotten everything about life except how to play the slots.

'So, you saw the lights up on the Ridge?' Mike stubbed out the cigarette in a tinfoil ashtray.

There was a notebook between us and one of those pens with all the different colours at the top.

'Yes, a few weeks ago.' I was trying to sound relaxed.

Marcus was rocking on the seat; he kept looking around the room, rubbing his head and taking short, sharp sucks of his cigarette.

'What did you see? Describe it again.' Mike took up the pen.

And so I did. Marcus was kicking his leg against the table, creating a slight vibration and flicking ash on the seat. I moved the ashtray closer to him.

'And did you hear anything, when they were there?' Mike's eyebrows were raised.

'It was totally silent,' I responded.

'And did you feel anything like heat or a warm wind?'

Marcus and I looked at each other, impressed with his questions. I shook my head to indicate there had been no sound, nothing to suggest a motor or an engine.

'What do you believe it was?' he asked, leaving his pen down and drinking his coffee.

I noticed he had a faint tremor in his hand.

'I think it could be something supernatural,' I replied.

'Tell him –' Marcus nudged me – 'about the dream.'

I paused for a moment, unsure whether to go there and looked out the window.

'You had a dream. . .?' Mike's voice sounded incredulous.

I turned back to him. He briefly glanced at his watch.

'Yes, I have a gift for predicting things, seeing them before they happen,' I said calmly.

'And you dreamed about the lights?' He was now leaning over the table towards me, eyes wide.

I nodded.

'I saw the town, and the lights, and then the town disappeared. . . a wave, or a flood came over everything.'

'She did, she told me about it before the lights came,' said Marcus.

This was not actually true, but I let it go.

'And this, this has happened before, you have predicted things. . .?'

'Yes. Not every dream but some of them, since I was four or five,' I replied.

'I'd like to include this, your prediction, your dream about the lights, in my next story. Dr Seymour Black will be visiting, would you talk to him? He's been investigating other sightings.'

'Yes,' I replied. 'I think people need to take it seriously. It's important and I have a duty to let them know.'

Marcus turned to stare at me as if I had spoken out of turn.

'Who is Seymour Black?' he asked then.

'He is a psychiatrist with an interest in the supernatural,' Mike said impatiently. 'Have you seen them again, since that night in June?'

'No, but they are coming back again, tomorrow night I think.'

'How do you know?'

'I dreamed it, of course,' I replied.

Mike coughed and looked to Marcus and then back to me.

'The Ridge has a history of some weird shit,' he said suddenly.

Before I could ask him about this I saw Mr Bowen through the window, carrying a large bunch of flowers and heading for the café.

The bell above the door rang out then. Mike threw his eyes over my head as Mr Bowen made his way towards us.

'Natasha, your mother was looking for you and I told her I'd keep an eye out.' He was attempting a smile and moving from one foot to the other.

'I'm sorry, you are. . .?' Mike slowly folded his arms.

Mr Bowen's cheeks were red and he dropped the flowers to his side.

'He's not my father, don't worry, he's just staying for the summer, a lodger,' I said.

Mike looked uncomfortable and reached for his cigarettes. The thump of drums started somewhere down the seafront. Marcus put his hand on mine under the table and I smiled to reassure him that Mr Bowen was not a concern.

'Her mother, that's who you need to talk to. Natasha, we should get back,' said Mr Bowen.

There was something presumptuous in his air and the language he used which made me uncomfortable.

'I might come to the house then this week and speak to her,' said Mike, nodding to Mr Bowen. 'Nice flowers, by the way,' he added.

No one answered but I could feel dislike rising and swaying between all of them. I moved in the seat and Marcus reluctantly pushed along to let me out, then stood up and eyeballed Mr Bowen. They were almost the same height.

Mr Bowen opened the door and Marcus followed us out.

'I can walk you home.' He glanced at him with distaste.

'It's fine,' I said.

Marcus looked disappointed and with hands in pockets wandered back towards his shop. Mr Bowen and I walked towards the promenade. A few teenagers were hanging off the side of the bandstand, shouting. Their bikes lay in a tangle on the ground.

'He's a good friend?' he asked.

'Yes, that's Marcus. He owns the takeaway on the seafront – well, his mother does. They live there.' I pointed in the direction of it.

'That's nice. . . I'm sorry for barging in, just Elizabeth asked me and I felt I couldn't say no.'

We both knew it wasn't his place to come and get me, and if anyone was to blame for the whole thing it was my mother.

'You have to be careful though, people can twist things. They don't mean to but they look for the sensational side of the truth,' he added.

'I know, newspapers are a necessary evil.'

It was something my mother used to say in her arch and haughty way. As we climbed the steps to the house I stopped and turned to look at the sea. It was calm and the sky was shades of orange, grey and pink.

'You are very lucky to live here.' He had stopped too and signed deeply as he gazed at the view.

'The staring town, that's what my mother calls it.'

'Sometimes it's hard to appreciate things that are familiar,' he said, glancing at me.

'I love it,' I answered.

'That's good. So many people are unhappy, dissatisfied, think there is something better elsewhere.'

'Like you and the city.'

'Very true.' He laughed, folding his arms.

'Why can't you write there this summer?' I asked.

'I don't know really, I just needed to be here.'

I knew this to be true. He had been called, something had moved or changed in the universe and he had been sent to us. And for a very brief moment he seemed to be open and filled with a kind of abundance and he wanted to share the feeling of it with me – a great thing was happening to him and he needed to recognize it, describe it to someone else for it to be real, but then he remembered he could not.

'Everyone always says that, when they come here first. . . holidays are like a drug,' I replied. I wanted to puncture his delusion.

'Useful being able to see into the future,' he said.

'You shouldn't laugh at me.'

I was not surprised my mother had told him about my premonitions, there was something between them, I could feel it.

'I would never do that.' He looked back to the sea.

'Do you believe I saw the lights?'

'I would never presume to know what you saw that night but whatever it was, there might be a number of possible explanations.'

'This is not all there is, there are so many things we can't see but they are real,' I said, my hands gesturing to the sky and the sea.

He stayed looking out to the horizon, his profile neat and sculpted, his black hair blowing gently in the breeze. I've always thought he looked like someone else, but I have never been able to remember who it was. There was a familiarity to him that was there right from those first few days at the end of June, as if we had known him before.

'I wouldn't know, I tend to live by what I can see and touch,' he replied, smiling and turning to look at me again.

'But I do know.'

'I envy you then,' he said, walking slowly on to the gate.

'How do you explain love if you only believe in things you can see?' I called after him.

He didn't look back, but paused and caressed the long swaying grass at his side with his hand.

'You've got me there,' he answered.

'You shouldn't be afraid.'

'I'm not afraid.' He turned back, frowning.

'I think you are.'

His shoulders slumped slightly and he looked sad then, his eyes weary, and I suddenly knew everything about him, how nothing had turned out as he'd expected so he had run away to the sea to find my mother, but even his growing hope and wonder at her was tainted by age and exhaustion. He was falling in love and it would not be an easy thing.

'Let's go home, it's late.' He pushed open the narrow, rusting gate and entered the garden.

I watched him walk slowly along the gravel path in the twilight, his back hunched still, and I thought how he would need reminding that this wasn't his home. He was just this summer's paying guest.

Chapter Eight

The next morning my mother was up unusually early and had set up her easel at the edge of the orchard. There were jars of paint and water at her feet, the canvas bare. Her hair was tied up in a ponytail and she was humming. I watched her for a bit from the front step as she mixed her colours. She seemed different, her movements were lighter, quicker, they had a purpose. She was engrossed in the detail of setting things up but every now and then she stopped and just stared at the white canvas.

'I want to believe you, about the lights. . .' she said suddenly, not yet turning around.

There were bees above her head and she wafted them away with her hand.

'I'm sure,' I replied, walking over to her.

She reached out as if to touch my arm, but I pulled back. There were ants on my leg and I bent down to brush them off.

'You could have chosen a better moment to tell the newspaper. We need Mr Bowen to stay, and not have to be retrieving you from cafés at night,' she said.

'You sent him on that errand.'

She looked hot already, her forehead clammy and damp.

'Why do we need him to stay?' I asked.

'Money.' She bent down to mix some paint.

'Shouldn't you be slightly more concerned about the lights and what they are?'

'There is nothing I can do about it. If it's the end of the world, all I can do is drink and maybe smoke again.'

Flippancy, something she used when she wanted to escape reality.

'Don't joke about it,' I said and for a second I thought I might cry.

'Don't talk to that journalist again,' she replied.

'He's only reporting what people saw.' I wiped my forehead.

She stopped to take her hair down and redo it in a bun, a clip in her mouth.

'Just trust me on this. I believe you saw something but you shouldn't be telling everyone about it,' she said.

Was she as bohemian as I remembered? Perhaps it was all an act and really she wished I played tennis in the club like everyone else. I think about this a lot now, it is the endless riddle of our relationship. She pretended to be free, but wasn't.

'Do you want me to hide for ever?' I asked.

'You don't want the town talking about you. Besides, showing people who you really are is quite overrated, believe me.'

It was ironic, people did talk about us – we were endlessly conspicuous, despite our best efforts.

'I thought we were supposed to live authentic lives? I might have something very important to share with people,' I replied.

'There is authenticity and there is purposely creating drama, and scaring everyone, not the same.'

'I can't help that I dream things, see things.'

She took a deep breath. 'I know, it's just other people might not understand. I don't understand and I love you. It's not exactly a science that can be explained.' Then she looked at me seriously.

'Neither is this,' I said, pointing at the paints.

'I believe in expressing things.'

'I'm expressing something.'

She folded her arms and sucked in her lip, flicking her gaze back to the house, thoughtful suddenly.

'Lewis tried to talk to me about the lights yesterday. It was hard to understand him. He drew pictures of the Ridge, too,' she said.

I kicked one of the small green apples that had dropped off the tree too early.

'His mother rang me about it last night, she says he is very restless, can't sleep and wants to stay at the window all night looking at the sky.'

'She'll probably try and drag him to those doctors again. She should just listen to him, he understands.'

'Oh, I hope she doesn't do that,' she replied, looking worried.

'Lewis has seen them and other people too. I can help to find out what it all means, and if there is a message for us. I am really the best person to try and understand. I can feel things, sense them.'

'Why do you think it makes you special?' she said. 'Perhaps the ability makes you different, unusual, cursed even.'

Her words seemed sharp and mean, a lessening of me.

'How long will Mr Bowen be staying?'

'Honestly, Natasha, please don't cause a fuss, you know this is how it is in the summers, we need a lodger and you can call him Seán.' She turned back to her canvas.

'How long?' I asked again.

'Until the end of August.'

'That long.'

There was the hum of wasps around us.

'I met him a few months ago, before he came to stay, at a gallery in the city,' she said, suddenly looking out through the trees towards the edge of the cliff.

It all made a sort of terrible sense. I stopped scratching the bites, there was blood on my nails.

'I should have told you before he came.' She turned back to me.

That air of inevitability again, things falling into place, being determined, like I had felt with Mr Bowen on the cliff steps the night before. I didn't speak for a minute and showed her the blood on my nails. She looked briefly at my scratched and bitten legs and then took a tissue out of her pocket and handed it to me.

'There is nothing unusual about it.' The leaves created a dapple of light on her lovely face.

'Isn't there?'

I had to get away from her then and walked back to the house. The smells and sounds of the garden seemed amplified and intense, intoxicatingly sweet, and the sky was a deep, deep blue, bare of all clouds. Mr Bowen had dragged the garden chair into the shade at the side of the front door. I could see the yellow marks on the grass from where it had stood originally. He had kicked out his long legs and was reading a book. There was a glass of what looked like my mother's cordial and an ashtray on the ground beside him. It was an affront to see him there so comfortable. The cat was lying close by, she raised her head as I approached.

'Natasha,' he sat forward in a jerky, surprised fashion.

As he spoke he accidentally kicked the glass with his foot and it overturned, sweet liquid leaking over the gravel. I noticed the book he was reading, *The Fall* by Albert Camus, one of my mother's favourites. The cat jumped up, alert now, her ears pinned back.

'Aren't you supposed to be writing? You never seem to be,' I said.

'You caught me, again.' He smiled and looked down, about to reach for the glass.

'She has had other boyfriends, you know,' I said, standing almost over him.

He lifted his head, everything about him slow now.

'And not just my father.'

I felt my cheeks turning red, sweat in the middle of my back. He stayed looking at me but didn't say a word. I was aware that I was embarrassing myself and being cruel but somehow I couldn't stop the words from coming.

Were there so many men? my therapist asks me now. I mostly try and forget, they came and they went. It was never serious. Some were nice to me, bought me a toy or an ice cream, some of them pretended I wasn't there. She never hid them, nor did she speak of them much either. They too were filed away in the silence. They never lasted long, drifted into our lives for a month or two, an unfamiliar car parked at the side of the house, an extra wine glass upturned in the sink. She always acted as if they didn't matter much, they were a necessary inconvenience, until Mr Bowen.

'Natasha, no more.' My mother had followed me.

What was I afraid of? the therapist asks me. Becoming less in her eyes, being unloved, displaced, abandoned. I was old enough to know better in a way, but then she had never been in love before and it unsettled me. The idea of her wanting something more than what we had, something more than me, was disconcerting. I sensed change all around me and the power of something elemental and huge coming, like a wave that was going to pull her far away from me.

There was coughing behind us and I jumped. It was Marcus at the gate.

I gestured to him and we went into the house. My mother and Mr Bowen said nothing as we passed but the air was thick with anger. Marcus sat at the kitchen table, while I got juice from the fridge. He looked hot, faintly sunburned. I gave him the glass and he drank it quickly.

'Do you have any ice?' he asked.

I got him some cubes from the freezer, put them in a cup and he placed one on the back of his neck. It started to melt on touching his skin. He leaned back relieved, his eyes closed briefly.

'The other kids are afraid of you,' he said then, putting the dripping, melting cube down on the table.

He had orange peel on the corner of his lips and his eyes looked aquamarine; his hair pushed back had freed them and they sparkled in the bright white of the kitchen.

'I don't care really, they are mean.'

'Not all of them, some are nice, and you do actually care,' he said.

'I don't.'

'You liked it when they looked at you, listened to you. The way you like it when you tell me things you have dreamed. I saw it on the beach,' he said, putting his arms behind his head and smiling.

'I just felt like nobody takes anything important seriously, like Lewis was getting hurt and no one cared, and the lights – people are just chatting about it like it's a football match or something. It's important and they need to understand, someone needs to help them understand,' I replied.

'People just do their own thing sometimes and we don't know that the lights are important yet, almost no one has actually seen them anyway.'

This irritated me greatly.

'You should have helped Lewis yesterday,' I answered.

His eyes opened wide and he looked surprised, embarrassed, and folded his arms across his chest. He wasn't wearing his father's bracelet any more.

'I didn't know what to do,' he answered, frowning.

'Where's your bracelet?' I asked, touching his wrist.

He looked down at my hand and then up at me.

'I was afraid I would lose it.'

We didn't say anything for a second, just stared at each other.

'Lewis freaks me out, he's always watching us,' he said then, glancing out the window.

'He's just different.'

'And everyone was looking, I just couldn't get involved. I don't want trouble,' he replied.

'You have to stand up for people sometimes,' I said.

'I don't have to.' He rolled the empty glass to the edge of the table.

I didn't know what to say to that.

My mother dropped something then outside, we heard her curse. Marcus got up suddenly, pushed the chair back and went to the window, resting his head against the glass. I noticed there were more dead flies on the windowsill, and I brushed them onto the floor.

'I didn't know she was painting again,' he said.

'She wanted to be a painter, but then she had me and everything got messed up. She tries again every few years.'

He turned from the window to look at me. 'Don't say it like that,' he said, shaking his head.

'Like what?'

'Like it's your fault.'

'It's the truth, I've made my peace with it,' I answered, pretending I was cool about all these things.

'What were you fighting about outside?'

'Mr Bowen, the lights, me generally. She doesn't want me to say I've seen them, doesn't want me to talk about my gift or anything.'

He rubbed his head.

'Tell people to come to the Ridge tonight,' I said.

'Who?'

'Your new friends – on the beach.'

He blushed and kicked the wall under the window. Mr Bowen was standing beside my mother looking gloomily at her empty canvas, hands in his pockets.

'I think he likes her,' said Marcus.

He pressed his hand to the window; his sweat left an outline on the pane and I felt a strained energy and yearning in him forcing itself against the cool of the glass.

'Why do you say that? He looks miserable out there,' I responded sharply.

He shrugged his shoulders but stayed watching them. 'Maybe you will get a new dad,' he said softly.

I could see the little white fishing boat rounding the Ridge, Marcus and Lewis playing somewhere, not understanding that everything was about to change.

'Women can want more than a husband, we just need his money for the summer,' I answered.

'What do you want?' he asked.

I could feel his gaze on me again, the heat of the sun coming off his body, staining the glass with his sweat. And I couldn't think what to say. I want people to listen to me, understand me, would perhaps have been the most honest of answers. I see things – believe me.

His gaze retreated to the garden as his hand left the window and fell to his side.

I stayed watching my mother who was now animatedly explaining something about her blank canvas to Mr Bowen. She was rarely animated, it must have been driven by nerves, trying to make up for my outburst. He was looking at her intensely, listening, deciding whether to stay or not, weighing it all up, and his head was a chaos of guilt and desire. I could feel it from this distance.

'Lewis thinks he's going to die. He told me yesterday,' I said.

'He doesn't know what he's talking about.'

'That's not true,' I said. 'I've dreamed about him slipping away from me, underwater.'

I didn't say I had seen Marcus in that dream too, both of them drifting into a great flood.

'I have to protect him,' I said, turning away from the window.

This would become my burning mission in a way, that and getting rid of Mr Bowen.

Chapter Nine

Word slowly spread among the teenagers in the town that there was something unusual expected that night. Graffiti of an alien with giant eyes was spray-painted on the side of one of the bars and Lewis was seen sitting cross-legged on the beach looking up to the sky, his face ghostly in the evening light. It was claimed that he was worshipping sky gods and some kids threw plastic bottles at him. Mike Ryan was spotted with a notebook and a beer in one of the restaurants along the shoreline, a man with a camera beside him in the booth. It was still a joke though to most people, some harmless fun in the sun.

The night air was cool on my face as I ran from the house close to ten that night and met Marcus outside his shop. There was music coming from the bars on the seafront and a lone girl danced in the street as we sped past, heading for the Ridge. Reedy, dry grass moved in the night breeze as we made our way into the forest and I could see the shadowy outline of a person smoking in the bushes, the hiss and orange dazzle of a lighter illuminating him briefly. Marcus kicked a can as we ran. It rolled under my foot and I crushed it. The path climbed higher and higher.

'Did anyone else come?' I called out, breathless.

'On the ledge,' he shouted back.

The gorse bushes were thicker now, closing in on us. The path narrowed and both of us stumbled on the sharp rocks embedded in the deep earth. We stopped a minute in a clearing in the trees and looked back to the town below, a thin curve of light in the bay, everything about it small, a doll's house of a place. Far away, down the coast, there was an orange haze in the sky that marked the start of the city.

We pushed on through the gorse and made our way along the edge of the Ridge, into a clump of trees. There were pines, thin, bent over, leaning away from the coast and looking deformed. I took Marcus's hand, it was sweaty and slippery. There was the thrashing of birds in the trees above our heads, a rush of urgent wings echoed in the darkness, something fell and landed at our feet and I jumped.

'A cone,' said Marcus. He was trying to sound unafraid but his voice wavered.

'Come on, come on. . . I'll lead you,' he said.

We walked on with Marcus as guide pulling me along. He made me feel safe, as if things would work out all right. I felt the breeze then, we had reached the ledge that hung over the sea, dark blue sky ahead, the moon hidden. There was one boy there waiting, and a girl, they had lit a small bonfire of twigs and were sitting in the sandy grass.

'Some of the others were afraid, they wouldn't come. . .' said the boy, looking as if we might scold him.

'And some didn't believe you,' added the girl.

She was wearing a pink hoodie with the words OHIO STATE on it, her camera around her neck. She stood up as we sat down and walked to the cliff edge. There was the gentle roll and hum of the waves far below.

'One of the gamblers from the casino threw himself off there,' said Marcus.

I sensed he was trying to impress her and I sat up straighter, alert suddenly.

'Why?' she asked, turning back to look at him.

'He lost all his money,' he replied, shrugging his shoulders.

She looked thoughtful and serious in the firelight before turning back to the dark edge and the sea. Marcus had brought a can of beer he must have stolen from his mother and offered it to me, but I refused.

'What's going to happen?' said the boy, looking at me with large eyes.

'Just wait,' said Marcus, taking a swig of his beer and wiping his mouth.

'I'm Victoria and he's Charlie,' said the girl.

The boy looked at us furtively while Victoria raised the Polaroid camera over her head and took a picture of the stars before coming back from the ledge and sitting on the ground with us. Marcus watched her closely, a slight frown of interest on his face as if she was a new and compelling puzzle. There was the distant sound of a train pulling in, the screech of a brake.

Victoria stared up at the sky while Charlie kept turning his head quickly around him, as if he expected the bogeyman to emerge from the trees. Marcus was restless too, fidgeting with sticks and leaves, then yawning and rubbing his eyes. I sat hunched and tense watching the fire.

'My brother saw them, the lights, he was camping here,' Charlie said.

Marcus grunted and started stabbing a stick into the ground.

'Was he afraid?' I asked.

'Yes,' the boy answered.

'You and your mother never come to our party,' said Victoria suddenly.

It was only then that I recognized her, she came every summer with her family and stayed in a pink villa near the train station. She was a year younger than me and went to a fancy boarding school; my mother and I had been trapped in a queue behind her mother once at the supermarket and she had told us all about it. Her family had a party every August and it was true, we always got the invitation but never went. I think they mistakenly thought we had money because our house was big and had the best view of the sea. They were from the city, rich and glamorous with an au pair, the father roaring into town every Friday evening in his big car.

'We don't go to parties,' I said, looking at the sky.

'We never get an invite,' said Marcus.

Victoria gave him an impish, smug glance and he winked at her.

'Everyone watches your mother, I've noticed that. She's very beautiful, she could have been a model I'd say, when she was younger, not now though,' she said thoughtfully.

She was silent for a minute and stared into the trees. Charlie brushed something off his neck and then looked fearfully at the ground to see what it was that had been crawling on him.

'Almost everyone was in love with her,' I answered.

I knew this to be true though my mother never spoke of it. I would have liked to know what it felt like to be desired, to be the object of adoration. The world must have felt quite different, but she never seemed interested in telling me about it.

'I can imagine,' said Victoria.

Marcus drank some more beer and wiped his mouth.

'What do you think they are, the lights?' she asked.

'I think they are ghosts and they have come with a warning,' I replied.

I could feel Charlie and Marcus watching me, Victoria meanwhile was looking into the trees.

'The dead, here?' She gestured with her hands.

'The people who killed themselves,' I answered.

'Or aliens,' said Charlie.

'And you predict things too, you are a psychic?' she asked.

'Who told you that?'

'The boy, the strange one on the beach.'

'Lewis,' said Marcus.

'He's telling everyone,' she said.

It was surprising, he didn't talk to people much, certainly not the tourists, and I had never been really sure if he knew that about me. Marcus had said it to him one day when he had wanted to scare him, but I didn't think he had been listening. You could never be sure with Lewis.

We were silent then, there was the very distant hum of a beat from one of the bars far below and the rustle of some birds shuffling and restless, high above us. A kind of drowsy peace was descending and the trees seemed to be breathing out an ancient whisper. The fire sparked and crackled, the smoke smelled of pine and earth, and occasionally there was the click and flash of Victoria's camera. She lay the pictures out in a circle around her like cards. They looked white and shiny in the low light. The other boy stared out to sea.

'If you kill yourself you go to hell,' said Charlie, still thinking about the gambler who jumped from the ledge.

He was shivering and his voice went up and down. Victoria snorted and touched the surface of the photos one by one as if she was counting them.

'They were going to put up a fence at the ledge, to stop people jumping, but then they didn't. I expect it wouldn't work anyway. People come here to die, nothing will dissuade them,' I said.

Victoria looked up at me briefly as if she had a question to ask about the dead but then refrained.

'You could tell fortunes,' she said, looking at me again.

'It doesn't work like that really,' I said.

'Doesn't it?' she answered.

I could feel Marcus's gaze on me in the dark; the stabbing motions he was making with the stick had ceased and he was still, thoughtful.

'People pay to know how their life will turn out,' she said.

'But maybe they wouldn't like to hear what I have to say,' I answered, staring back at her.

She looked down at the ground.

'I wouldn't want to know,' said Marcus.

I smiled at him and he smiled back. Victoria noticed and sat forward. She will interrupt us, I thought. It was a fleeting feeling that escaped into the dark and so I let it go.

'What's my colour, my aura thing?' she asked.

'I can't tell,' I replied.

Victoria lit a cigarette and offered another to Marcus who took it and inhaled deeply. The smoke looked blue in the dark. I could feel him relax with the hit of the nicotine, his body easing, and he looked up at the stars.

'There is a wood in Romania where a small girl went missing, and five years later she just walked out of the forest, and she hadn't got any older. She was exactly the same as when she went in,' said Victoria suddenly.

'That can't be,' said Charlie.

'A myth, legend, whatever,' replied Marcus between draws of smoke.

'No,' said Victoria.

There was something of the sullen, spoiled child to her. I expected Marcus to throw his eyes to heaven – he didn't like princesses – but he didn't do that. She pleased him in some way, perhaps it was her tiny face that was like a pretty porcelain doll.

'It's this real place, I read about it and lots of weird shit happens there, like people get lost because their compass doesn't work, or they feel really anxious and kill themselves, and the trees are shaped like knots, they don't grow straight and scientists can't explain why and there is this clearing in the centre where nothing ever grows and blue lights were seen there, like a UFO, and they think that's why nothing grows there, it's this portal to another world,' she said.

'Every fairy tale has a forest,' said Marcus, stubbing out his cigarette.

'It'd be cool if it was true, but maybe it's not,' Victoria said, glancing at him.

'It must be getting really late,' said Charlie, looking fearfully at the sky.

'What age are you?' asked Victoria.

She managed to be languorous and insulting at the same time.

'Thirteen and I am allowed out till eleven in the summer,' he replied.

'You really must have such cool parents,' she said, sighing.

Marcus laughed, got up from the ground and stretched his arms above his head. Victoria watched him admiringly.

'What kind of tests do you think they do, if it is aliens and they take you?' the boy asked.

'They check your insides, remove things,' said Marcus.

He looked to Victoria for a reaction.

'Make you have alien babies,' answered Victoria, laughing.

Charlie moved quickly, kicking leaves and dust as he stood up. His eyes were huge and fearful, staring wildly into the now dark forest.

'I have to go,' he said, looking quickly from side to side.

Marcus folded his arms and whistled for a second.

'I might as well go too,' said Victoria suddenly.

She stood up and gathered her things. Marcus watched her again, her nonchalance and indifference as to how she was perceived something new and enticing to him. I sensed that she was not at all like the other holiday kids, though she pretended to be when it suited her. She seemed like a benign threat, if such a thing was possible.

'They don't seem to be coming,' she said, pointing upwards, and her tone was not accusatory, more disappointed.

She pulled up the hood on her top and climbed over my legs to get past. 'What do you think they might want, if it is ghosts?' She had stopped on the edge of the woods.

'Maybe they're lonely,' I said.

She looked at me and nodded sadly. They both disappeared into the trees then.

'Don't. . .' I called after them suddenly.

But it was too late, they were gone.

'Let them,' said Marcus.

We heard faint clapping then in the distance and some people shouting. Marcus went to the ledge and threw the empty can over the side. I could hear it knocking against the rocks on the way down.

'Some drunks on the beach,' he said.

He returned from the edge, poked at the fire with the stick then looked at me, his eyes hot and curious. We didn't say anything and he sat down beside me, our legs touching. I knew he was glad that we were alone.

'Will you visit your dad some time?' he said, looking at me sideways.

'Why are you asking that?'

He shrugged his shoulders. I felt chilly suddenly, the breeze had risen slightly and the trees moved above us.

'I might, maybe you can come with me, when we are older,'

I replied. 'We could go backpacking like on a train around Europe. People do that.'

He looked sad. 'You will have other friends then, the ones you meet in college, you'll go with them.'

'I doubt that,' I said.

'She wants me to take over the shop, but I won't,' he said, gesturing angrily in the direction of his mother and the town.

'Put your arm around me,' I replied.

It was perhaps the first of my adult sentences, I see it as that now. His arm, uncertain, went around my shoulders. The trees bent and creaked, no longer shadows but bright, white, like stripped bones, and the moon rose above the clouds. Marcus started to breathe deeply, I felt his body relax and melt into my side.

'Everything is awake, alive,' I said, looking at the dark trees.

His arm felt heavy, like a weight, and there were goose bumps along my skin. It was months since I had felt cold, one forgot what it felt like. I closed my eyes and listened to his breathing, the rise and fall of his body, his arm like an anchor holding me down. There were more shouts and calls from the seafront far below and there was a strange melody to the sound.

'It's like it's moving,' I said.

The ground felt as if it was vibrating underneath me, an energy to it.

'Close your eyes,' I said to him.

There was a musky smell of cigarettes on his skin, and beer on his breath.

'I can't,' he said.

'Do it, close them, feel it, put your hands on the ground,' I said.

'Feel what?'

'The earth is alive with souls and spirits, like those woods Victoria told us about.'

I took his hand and forced it down into the dry, cracked soil. There was a throb, a shudder deep below us, like a life force buried, and I wanted him to feel it.

'It's there,' I whispered in his ear.

He didn't answer but let me keep his hand pressed down in the hard dirt. I felt the beat of the earth through his skin.

'You must feel it,' I said.

He whispered something but I didn't hear. I knew he was looking at me, his mouth an inch away in the dark, a strain of tight, explosive energy to his body again, pulsating, just like the ground beneath us.

'Close your eyes, they are coming,' I said.

The breeze rose and very faintly whistled through the branches of the swaying trees and seemed to go in rhythm with our breathing, a gentle rise and fall. Marcus leaned closer.

'Let me,' he whispered.

'I can't yet.' His mouth so close to mine I felt like I could bite it.

I could never really accept joy, my mother said this to me in one of our many arguments in the years that followed, and she was right. I distrusted it quite completely, it made you vulnerable, hopeful, and then you would likely be disappointed. If I could go back I think Marcus and I should have stayed like that, his face against mine and our eyes closed. We could have lain there in the dirt together, it would have been a different kind of summer.

But instead I opened my eyes and over his shoulder I saw them, lights flickering and swaying in the forest, like small blue fires. They were high in the trees, dancing again, and there was a low hum in the air, coming not from them but from the ground beneath me.

'They are here,' I said, pushing him away abruptly.

Marcus stumbled backwards on the ground like someone in pain, his arms went around his head as if he wanted to protect himself, and even though I was starting to understand that I loved him, I needed to follow the lights more and so left him there on the ledge.

The forest was blue and alive behind him, filled with an ethereal sense of grace, and I walked alone into the trees to search for them. I expected him to follow but he didn't. The lights led me on deeper and deeper into the woods, flickering and turning, always just a small distance above me, and I believed they were the souls of the dead and the hopeless and they had come back to find me and scold me for not saving them. I could hear them whispering, asking me to follow, and then suddenly they were gone. It all went black and I was lost for a time, thick foliage catching at my feet and the air filled with the odour of rotting earth. For a brief moment I thought I heard Lewis, and I turned quickly thinking he was there behind me, but it was just the soft wind in the firs.

Eventually I heard Marcus calling and I made my way back to him.

JULY

Chapter Ten

Two days later there was another article in the local paper. The story of the lights was now beginning to grow and spread, no longer a completely fringe occurrence, and my own compulsion to explain them to everyone began to take over. It's a sort of arrogance to think you have something important to say and that you should be listened to; though my therapist disagrees when I say this, she believes I was expressing myself and that this indeed was a valid and worthy thing to do. But I have my doubts, many doubts. And in this way, as the years have passed, I have become more like my mother. I have cultivated an evasive silence of my very own.

```
Fireballs, Orbs or a UFO?
Mike Ryan
Mysterious, multiple bright lights were once
again witnessed over the 'Ridge', the second
time in as many weeks. The blue lights appeared
to hover before disappearing suddenly in the
```

evening sky. A small number of residents in the area claim to have seen the latest, strange occurrence and say it lasted for about a minute.

Quick to play down concerns, local councillor Martin Barry says it is likely to be an optical illusion or a weather event and he will not be contacting any national authorities on the matter.

A man who begs to differ is noted psychiatrist Dr Seymour Black who is conducting his own investigations. Dr Black made headlines two years ago with the publication of his book *Encounters with the Truth* in which he explores his own journey from sceptic to believer.

Dr Black's reputation has come in for scrutiny by some in psychiatric circles since the publication of the book, with former colleagues claiming he is bringing the profession into disrepute with his support for those who claim to have experienced extraterrestrial and supernatural encounters.

'In the interviews I have conducted with people who say they have witnessed or experienced unusual phenomena, I generally do not find mental illness. I have found trauma,

```
but also authenticity and truth.'
    If you have seen anything strange in the
sky, contact this reporter.
```

* * *

I stood on the low wall of the promenade, outside Marcus's shop. I could see him inside cleaning the counters. He hadn't noticed me yet. A few people eating ice creams looked at me as they walked past. Babies were crying in buggies or leaning down to try and touch the sandy pavement with their soft toys. I coughed quietly to clear my throat, and then again a bit louder. The sun was sharp and I wished I had worn a hat. My hands were slippery with sweat and I wiped them on my shorts. I looked furtively from one side of me to the other, praying my mother would not be passing.

'I saw the lights on the Ridge,' I called out.

I felt my eyes waver and rubbed them. The air was dense again, heavy like a weight bearing down on my head. Some of the kids from the beach pulled up on their bikes, they stayed astride them watching me while sucking their ice pops. Lewis had wandered over from the bandstand to sit at my feet. He looked up at me, his face earnest. He had a book in his hand and was trying to show it to me. I had to shake my head and put my fingers on my lips to him. Marcus was at the window of the shop now, staring out.

'They are a warning from the dead.' My voice louder now.

A few people laughed, though the crowd kept growing. Some tourists with sun hats and caps stood looking at me, their hands on their hips as if I was some new form of entertainment and they were ready to be unimpressed.

'I heard they were aliens,' a man shouted.

Marcus had opened the shop door and was standing leaning against it, a cloth still in his hand. A tall, distinguished-looking man in a cream suit and a panama hat joined the crowd. Mike Ryan stood beside him, and they whispered to each other.

'I want to understand them and try and save us, if I can,' I said.

The sirens of the amusements started up then and the air felt like a giant, hot breath on my neck.

'You couldn't save anyone,' some people laughed.

'What do we need saving from?' called another.

There was a woman on the path, with fair hair, a scarf wrapped around her very tanned shoulders and large black sunglasses. She waved her arms at me and pushed roughly through the crowd.

'Witches walk among us,' she said, pointing her finger at me.

She had a leather shoulder bag, stuffed with home-made flyers. The crowd went silent.

'Do not be fooled by false prophets, shaman.' She thrust one in my hand, her eyes alight.

Lewis stood up, afraid, and climbed over the wall onto the sand. Marcus moved from the door swiftly and began walking to the front of the crowd. I knew he would rescue me if I needed it, but the woman passed on quickly, offering leaflets to other people as she went away towards the Ridge end of the beach. People parted to let her pass and Marcus didn't come to me, but stopped and watched her go.

'If anyone else has seen the lights, talk to me,' Mike shouted into the crowd.

'What kind of saving?' the man shouted again.

I didn't know what to say, from the end of the world maybe.

I looked down to the crumpled leaflet the woman had handed me.

There will be terrible times in the last days. People will be lovers of themselves, lovers of money, boastful, proud, abusive, disobedient to their parents, ungrateful, unholy, without love, unforgiving, slanderous, without self-control. . .

Lewis climbed back over the low wall and cupping his hand around his mouth whispered in my ear.

'They don't listen.'

He smelled of salt and seaweed.

* * *

I left the promenade quickly and went to the hotel where a meeting had been organized by Councillor Barry to try and reassure the town traders – there had been some disquiet after the article in the paper. The function room was hot, the windows were open to the seafront, but the air remained stifling and smelled of sweat. The man in the cream suit was seated at the front, with Mike beside him. He was Dr Black - Jim Lacey, the owner of the caravan park, had told me when I sat down.

'He's supposed to be an expert,' Jim said, throwing his eyes to heaven.

My mother arrived soon after me. The hotel manager greeted her like a special VIP guest but she barely acknowledged him, and scanned the crowd for me, squeezing past people in the row. A group of other local business owners arrived, grabbed some biscuits and sat in the chairs nearest the door. There was a low murmur of chatter, subdued and secretive. Some people who had seen me outside turned to look at us. My mother gazed down at her lap. She had brought an old copy of the *Reader's Digest*, a magazine she disliked but whose subscription she had failed to cancel, and was idly flicking the pages.

Councillor Barry emerged from a door near the podium. He looked scrunched up, his black suit creased, and his thinning hair was uncombed and wispy. There was a nervous head-twitching essence to him. He raised his hands to the room and coughed.

'Ladies and gentlemen, ladies and gentlemen, please.'

We went silent surprisingly quickly. His cheeks were red, he pulled at his tie and took a long drink of water. I looked to the door – Lewis had arrived. He had some red flowers in his hand, stolen from one of the cottages near the train station.

'I did not want to hold this meeting,' Councillor Barry said.

A murmur went through the room and I noticed a wasp hovering above the head of a woman in front of me.

'I feel it is just adding fuel to the nonsense that is being spread about ghosts, aliens and lights,' he continued. 'There is such a thing as an optical illusion, like electrics and dust in the air and that sort of thing.' His eyes were wide and staring now and he pointed at the crowd.

'So you admit there are lights of some kind, then?' said Jim.

My mother used the *Reader's Digest* to fan herself.

'I am not one to deny the words of any concerned person in this town. But I know that what might be a genuine account of some kind of aerial phenomenon is being used, twisted even,' said Councillor Barry.

As he spoke, he gazed at Dr Black. One of the men who ran the casino clapped briefly and then stopped. Dr Black raised his hand as if to ask a question, but the councillor ignored him.

'It's important we stick together as a community, we must not be divided by people who will try and divide us over this matter,' he said.

It didn't sound right, a faltering call to arms. I turned to look at Lewis who was picking some petals off the flowers and throwing them on the floor and smiling. The manager of the hotel glared at him and whispered in the ear of the receptionist.

'Well, if it's not anything extraterrestrial, are you going to find out what it is?' asked one of the men who ran the amusements.

'Anyone heard of the Marfa lights?' said someone behind us.

The councillor wiped his forehead with a bright red handkerchief. Lewis walked over to our seats and, reaching across some startled people, gave my mother the petal-less flowers. She touched her neck briefly before taking them and thanking him. The hotel manager moved quickly, took Lewis by the arm and led him out of the door.

'We will be monitoring and talking to the relevant meteorological bodies to see if they can explain the situation, also to the coastguard. But I tell you now, pay no heed to rumours, we cannot have this kind of fear-mongering.' The councillor waved his hands at the room.

He drifted into tourism speak and his eyes had a glaze to them. A woman raised her hand high in the air and began waving it furiously.

'Some of my guests are nervous, their son saw the lights out camping, what should I say to them? I don't think we can dismiss concerns as easily as you suggest.' She glanced to the people either side of her.

'It could be the Russians monitoring,' said a man who ran a grocery store.

There was an intake of breath and people started chatting amongst themselves. I heard someone mention nuclear fallout, and the red sand.

'They came before, you know,' said Jim.

This news was met with a hushed silence.

'People will not remember but they were seen before, many years ago when I was young.'

I stood up suddenly, my chair jerking back into the person behind me. 'I saw them the other night, they are real.'

Everyone turned to look at me. My mother grasped my hand and tried to pull me down into my seat, while also attempting to apologize to the man behind us whom the chair had knocked against. People started to speak amongst themselves, panic and tension rising.

Dr Black rose and turned to me. He was not a man you would forget. He looked like an ageing matinee idol, something from a black-and-white film that you might watch on a rainy Sunday afternoon. Tall and broad but with a very elegant face, slanting black brows, fine, high cheekbones and greying hair. He must have been in his sixties or so.

'What do they want?' someone shouted.

My mother pulled again on my arm, urging me to sit down.

'It's a warning,' I said.

A murmur of disquiet passed through the room. Dr Black signalled politely to me to sit down.

'Some of you may know who I am, but for those who don't, I am Dr Seymour Black. I am a psychiatrist with an interest in the paranormal. I am here not to create or stir up rumours as has been suggested, but instead to meet with those who have been affected by these unusual occurrences.' He nodded at me.

His voice was mellow and solemn and carried right to the back of the room.

'I believe there has been some activity which cannot yet be explained. It follows a pattern of other sightings in the region over the last forty or fifty years. I think for those who are concerned, you should not be. In my experience, which I should add is quite significant, these types of sightings happen more frequently than people are willing to admit. It does not mean we should be alarmed, but we should be vigilant and show understanding, particularly to those who claim to have seen something,' he said.

'I am staying here in the hotel for the next while and will be very happy to talk to anyone who wishes to do so. We should be open and curious, rather than paranoid or frightened.' Then he sat down.

I felt filled with light and relief – finally someone who would understand. The audience was silent for a minute before hands darted up. Councillor Barry returned to the podium.

'Anyone who has concerns, talk to me,' he said.

Mike raised his hand with a question.

'Not you,' the councillor answered and left the podium, moving to the window.

The hotel manager rushed to his side and spoke in his ear. People started to get up and wander out in twos and threes. My mother stayed rigid in the seat, looking ahead, the *Reader's Digest* held in mid-air. She couldn't bear to look at me. Dr Black walked over to us. He was a giant of a man but he moved with finesse through the room, dodging people who tried to reach for him effortlessly. His eyes when they stopped on me were bright with curiosity. He greeted my mother like an old-fashioned gentleman, almost bowing his head. She stood up then and put the magazine tightly under her arm.

Dr Black gestured to the councillor, an eyebrow raised. 'Men who profess to be shepherds to their people, rarely are.' Then he looked briefly down at her hand, the dead flowers crumbling.

I felt my cheeks burn, there was so much I wanted to say.

'What is it you want?' my mother asked.

'To speak to your daughter,' he replied quietly, nodding to me.

'We are not interested in being part of this circus,' she said.

I gripped the back of the seat in front of me.

'Mrs Rothwell, I'm afraid you already are,' he replied.

'Not by choice. Please excuse me.' Her cheeks were flushed

and she walked haughtily away to the door, leaving a trail of dead leaves on the floor.

Dr Black touched my arm briefly as I went to follow her.

'Natasha, do not listen to the disbelievers,' he said. 'In my experience most prophets are derided – until they can't be any more.'

Chapter Eleven

The seafront was dense with bodies in the days that followed, the intense heat of that July ripening the mood. It made some people drowsy, a lethargy in their bones as they walked from beach to café, dragging themselves along; others glowed with a simmering energy. Men had mottled, sore skin, slick with sweat, their caps worn backward to protect raw necks. Thin boys took their tops off, and dived from the rocks of the Ridge into the dark green water; girls clapped their efforts before sliding into the sea after them like sleek seals. Mothers sat on the beach with picnic baskets, their children escaped to the water.

There were fights in the bars in the evenings, we could hear breaking glass and shouts from our garden and then later, much later at night, there were electric storms, spectacular pyrotechnic displays. One of the storms lit a fire on the Ridge that took two days to put out; smoke filled the air above the town and made the sky a strange hazy mauve colour. No one could sleep and people watched the night sky with a growing sense of unease and some wonder. Everyone had heard about the lights now.

Dr Black stayed away from our house over the next two days, though he was a noticeable presence in the town, his large green car parked outside the hotel and a stream of people going to speak to him. Not just the few who had seen the lights, but others who wanted to talk about strange and mysterious things that happened in the town years before, occurrences we had all dismissed as just coincidences or random events. The child that went missing one Halloween, the suicides on the Ridge, the dead flies. . . it was a cornucopia of doom and oddness. All the folk tales of the town came back to life.

Mr Bowen seemed to forgive my outburst in the garden earlier in the week and I didn't speak of other men to him again. My mother attempted to make some new vegetarian meals with a Moroccan theme. They were spicy and hot and Mr Bowen gulped copious amounts of water at the table and insisted they were delicious. She didn't speak about the meeting in the hotel, she didn't want to know what I had seen on the Ridge.

'It might have been a meteor shower,' Mr Bowen said as we finished dinner that night. He looked at me with his serious, thoughtful eyes, willing me to open up.

'I don't want to talk about it,' I replied.

My mother gazed out the window, a wine glass in hand. 'Jim said they came before, many years ago.' She spoke in a distracted, dreamy way.

Mr Bowen looked interested, he laid his glass down on the table. 'Perhaps there were reports in newspapers at the time, we could check in the library,' he said.

'I wonder what the warning was then?' She ignored him and looked at me.

I got up from the table and dumped my plate loudly in the sink.

'And whether it came true.' Her voice faded off as I left the room.

* * *

Marcus was busy working most days but would spend the evenings with me hanging around the promenade or lying under the trees in the orchard of our garden. In the week after the latest sighting he didn't talk about what had happened between us or why he hadn't been able to look up at the lights that night. It bothered him, I knew, but he couldn't explain what had happened, or where his courage had gone, so he acted tough instead. He seemed to kick things more, jump off high walls, slice the backs of his legs sliding down rocks, cut his hand on broken glass on the beach. His movements had a kind of wild snarling anarchy to them, his eyes darting and restless.

We were followed by some of the holiday kids, the boys on bikes, swerving and swaying between us, their expressions curious. Occasionally Victoria would hang out for a bit, eating candyfloss, with heart-shaped sunglasses perched on her head. She was impeccably cool and used sarcasm as an armour so you were never quite sure what she thought of you. Lewis would be there too, but on the edges, standing with his bike, watching.

They all wanted to know when the lights were coming back and whether we were all going to be abducted, or if it meant the end of the world. I was a macabre attraction and I felt special in a way. The attention reminded me of the throb I had felt in the earth on the Ridge that night. There was an invisible beat underneath everything and everyone, and it either went in your favour or against. There could be a thrill in having the eyes of others on you, I had never thought that before. But at that particular moment, I wondered if this was what my mother had felt all her life, and if so why she had not enjoyed it more?

Despite this, I didn't speak much to them, they were intimidating in their city language and ways. They talked with an innate blistering, sunburned sort of confidence made of money and self-belief. I didn't need to speak much anyway, the story about me was growing and expanding without my even needing to take part. I had predicted deaths, accidents, lost swimmers at sea, knew where the bodies of the missing were buried and who would die young. I was the girl of dreams, visions, lights, tea leaves and palms. And I felt relieved in a way, like something I had hidden about myself was now free.

Marcus was quiet around them when I was there, a wary but curious look in his eye. He took their gifts, the odd cigarette or a can of beer, the spoils of these new friendships. One night he got drunk. I was in the garden reading when I heard my name being called faintly. I went to the gate and he was sitting on the steps halfway down the cliff, a can in his hand, and blood on the side of his cheek, strands of his blond hair stuck to it. He had tripped on the steps. I ran to get a cloth from the kitchen and wiped the blood away from his hot face. He closed his eyes at my touch and his eyelids looked delicate, the dark lashes thick and damp.

'What's going to happen?' he said, his words slurred as he opened his eyes to mine.

He smelled of beer, there were stains on his T-shirt and his hands were filthy, dirt under broken nails. I gently dabbed the side of his face some more.

'Are they coming for someone?' His eyes were serious.

He touched the cut on his cheek and then looked out to sea, his fair hair blowing in the warm evening breeze. The sky before us was huge, endless, a deep pink colour subsiding into red.

'It's hard to explain,' I said.

I closed my eyes and suddenly I could see Marcus in my head walking as a small boy with his father on the Ridge, the light golden, grasses blowing, birds swooping over their heads and the sea shimmering in the distance. Marcus scampering around trees and bushes, peeping his head out, but then I could feel his fear, and it was as if a light had gone off. His father was out of sight, gone, and panic was setting in. It was dank and dark, the grass wet and water dripping off the trees, his father fading, turning translucent in the twilight.

'My dad. . .' he said.

I opened my eyes – I had read his mind. I felt like a thief able to steal away inside him.

'I can see him, he is near you but he doesn't say anything. The dead never speak to me,' I answered.

I felt his gaze on me. He used to make me feel as if I had no errors and was made not of ordinary things but of magic, and that it was marvellous. I have never felt that way since.

'Why not?' he asked.

'They don't want to talk.' I rested my hand on his warm arm.

He rubbed his eyes and put his head down and picked at some of the lichens on the steps.

'What does he look like?' he asked.

'He looks young. He loves you, but he can't find you. . . he keeps looking for you though,' I replied.

Marcus sobbed then and put his hands over his head as if shielding himself from a blow. I hugged him to me, tucking my head under his chin. He felt famished, starved almost, and desperate to be filled with something, love I suppose now.

'They are always here, the dead. . . I need to tell you something.' I spoke into his neck.

He pulled away and looked down at me; one of his eyes was bloodshot and red-rimmed and he seemed broken in ways I hadn't seen or understood before.

'I was in the garden here, the day your dad's boat went out. I watched it, I knew it wasn't coming back.'

A flicker of disbelief and pain went across his face and he started to cry again. I reached up to touch his cheek. It felt hot and there was stubble near his chin, his skin raw and uneven. I was glad I had told him, he needed to know. We were closer than he could ever have imagined, united in a moment that changed both our lives though we had not known it at the time. It was perhaps why I always felt there was something deep, essential between us. I too had lived with the pain of his greatest darkness, it had entwined us and the universe understood we needed to be together.

'Stay with me.' He leaned his head against mine.

We didn't say much after this, there was no need. I took his hand and we watched the still sea and the white birds that flew in from the coast and soared high above us. I understood his silence that night to be love. It was the last time I would ever feel that and when I think about it now, I see it as a moment that marked the end of innocence. I thought we had been chosen, like two characters in a fairy story, filled with unease and uncertainty at the strange fate handed to us, a dangerous journey ahead, and we had to trust each other. There was something connecting us for ever, a loss both predicted and felt.

But I was wrong, profoundly so.

* * *

A few nights later there was a bonfire on the beach. The kids from the city had gathered wood from the Ridge, the fire sparked and groaned as the breeze picked up and the air smelled like burned sugar. There was beer stashed in a plastic bag and cigarettes were handed around, there was the faint tinny sound of music from a mini-radio. Marcus was kicking a ball with some of the other boys, they shouted and roared, diving into the sand, restless shadows moving in the twilight. Victoria was sitting on her own facing out to sea.

'I wish I'd stayed longer with you the other night on the Ridge,' she said quietly.

I picked up pebbles on the beach beside her.

'I wanted to, but then I was afraid and now I have missed something huge – were you scared?' She looked at me.

'There really isn't any point in being frightened,' I said. 'When something is bigger than you, or more powerful, you just have to accept it.'

'You must be particularly calm. I would like to be but never am, it's annoying,' she said.

'People always think they can control things, like I feel it when they talk, they are always fighting something, and maybe they should just give in.'

'You can see into people's heads?'

'Not exactly, but I sense what they are feeling.'

'That is like a superpower. So you know when someone is lying?' she asked.

'No, I just might feel wary of them.'

'And what am I feeling?' she asked.

'Bored and. . .'

She laughed then.

'And what?' she said, eyebrows sharply raised.

I had a sudden sense of blackness around her, as if she had been removed, like the outline of a picture you cut out from the pages of a magazine. Disembodied and without context.

'It's nothing, I can't. . .' I fumbled for an answer, digging my hand into the cool, damp sand.

I didn't trust her.

'Are they coming back, the lights?' She traced some shapes in the sand.

'I think they will, it's not finished,' I replied.

Marcus and one of the other boys had stopped playing and they were drinking from the cans, spilling beer on their T-shirts and laughing, pushing each other down onto the sand.

One of the other boys led a girl away to the rocks at the foot of the Ridge. Marcus stilled suddenly and watched them walk into the shadows. I felt an alarm of sorts go off in my head and stared at his profile, willing him to come and sit with me.

'What do you feel about Marcus?' Victoria asked.

'What do you mean?' I dragged my eyes away from him.

'What is he thinking?' she said.

One of the other boys had put their arm around Marcus and they whispered to each other, then started to laugh.

'I can tell you – he likes her, very, very much,' whispered Victoria, pointing to the caves.

I was not sure what to think, she was most surely mistaken. It seemed somehow impossible. Why was I so surprised? It amazes me now really. I was blind to the things that were obvious, forever seeking meaning in the cracks, in the shadows, and missing that which lay openly in the sun.

'They all talk about her, and honestly you would lose faith listening to them, it's not in the least bit romantic at all,' she said, smacking the sand.

'Who is she?'

'Oh, just someone here on holiday.' Victoria shrugged.

I turned to the Ridge and strained my eyes in the low light to try and see her, but she had disappeared. 'How do you know Marcus likes her?'

'It's obvious. He's always talking about her, and looking at her. You don't need a superpower gift to see that. I think it might be her breasts.' She laughed then.

I looked back to Marcus, he was pushing the other boy, trying to get the ball from him. I couldn't think of anything to say or do to get him to leave them and sit beside me. I turned to the cave but there was no sign of the girl. One of the boys started shouting suddenly behind us and pointing to the sea where Lewis was walking along the waterline, his hat under his arm.

'Stop creeping around and spying on us, freak,' another of the boys called out.

Victoria continued to trace the sand with her fingers and didn't look up. Marcus had stopped messing and was scanning the reactions of the others; his eyes finally rested on me before moving away quickly to the Ridge.

'Don't say that,' I shouted.

The boy was unsteady on his feet, beer spilling on the sand, the fire growling behind him as he walked slowly towards me.

'He's the fucking devil, and you're a witch.' He pointed at me.

Victoria breathed in sharply but stayed playing with the sand, not looking up. Marcus bent down, picked up his can and walked back to the other boys and the football.

'You don't know what you're talking about,' I said.

Marcus would come surely and defend both me and Lewis.

'There are things up there.' I gestured to the Ridge looming above the beach.

They were all silent now, the ball forgotten on the sand.

'The lights, they mean darkness,' shouted Lewis, walking towards me.

The street lights of the promenade reflected in his face, he looked blue and orange.

'I'm *so* scared,' said one of the boys, mimicking a girl's voice.

'Don't listen to this crap, he doesn't even make sense. If it's a light. . . it's not dark.' The mean boy shouting turned to look at the others.

'Let's go to the Ridge now, we can prove there's nothing there,' he shouted.

But no one moved for a second, except Marcus who sat down on the sand and watched me calmly over his can. The boys, as if taking their cue from him, picked up the ball again and started playing – they would stay on the beach. I stood up quickly and walked after Lewis. He had veered away from the shore and our group and was walking quickly in the direction of the Ridge.

'Wait,' I called after him.

He had put his black hat on and pulled it down low, almost covering his eyes.

'Don't go up there,' I said, stopping in front of him.

He looked down at the sand. I could feel a nervous energy in him, like a startled child, or animal even. 'It's quiet,' he said.

'It's not safe, I feel it, here,' I said, punching my chest.

He looked up at me then, and I thought he might cry, his eyes were wet and shining.

'I've had dreams,' I said. 'You know the way I have them and I see things and I think it's not safe up there for you. I will try and understand the lights, Dr Black is going to help me. You don't have to, you just need to wait and be safe at home.'

'I don't sleep any more,' he said sadly.

'I know, but I will take you home tonight. It's better not to go to the Ridge, please trust me,' I repeated.

We walked back to his house along the promenade which was busy, some people drinking and sitting in the twilight on the walls; Marcus's takeaway was thronged with a queue lined up outside – his mother had hired in extra staff. The town was spilling over with day trippers, as well as the usual holidaymakers. Many of them had come especially to see the lights. A young man with a doll of ET under his arm skateboarded past us; an elderly couple were out for a night stroll, the man had a cane and he raised it in greeting as we passed. Lewis stopped to watch him go.

'I'd like one of those,' he said.

We kept walking, cutting up through a lane that led off the seafront to the fishermen's cottages. The music from the bars began to fade away behind us. His mother thanked me when we arrived at the door and asked me in, offering me ice cream which I declined because it was late. She was quite a bit older than my mother, her hair short and greying, glasses on a chain around her nack and a puzzle book under her arm. She looked in a way as mothers were supposed to look, worn out, their lives finished somehow. My mother was quite different, she looked like her life had never really started.

'I do them in the evenings,' she said, noticing my gaze.

'We got a crossword book once because we like reading and we thought we would be good at them but we were useless, it's the same with Scrabble.' I spoke nervously.

Lewis was gesturing to the door of his bedroom which was at the back of the cottage. As I went to follow him his mother gripped my arm tightly.

'Thank you,' she said, her eyes sad.

Lewis's room was lit by a small lamp, the tiny window was wide open and the curtains blew gently inward. He stood near the bed and held his arms out from his side, willing me to look – on each of the four walls were his drawings of ghostly figures with giant eyes and devils with pitchforks. They were staring, almost leaning down over us, their fiery gazes fixed and unforgiving.

'Oh, Lewis,' I said, sinking onto the bed.

The room felt heavy, smothered in anxiety and dry heat.

Chapter Twelve

Dr Black called the next morning. We were in the garden, the parasol was propped against the wall, ready to be unfurled should we finally give in to the torment of the high sun. The cat lay sprawled in the shade of the porch. My mother was painting under one of the apple trees, and Mr Bowen was reading, while I lay on a scratchy blanket, occasionally flicking ants away.

Dr Black wore his white panama hat and another of his summer suits, this one a very pale green. He looked ice cool, impervious to the high sun.

'I believe you have a very special daughter,' he said, his voice clear and authoritative.

I felt myself going red, while Mr Bowen sat upright sharply in his chair, his work laid down on the ground.

'She has witnessed something out of the ordinary, and it forms part of a pattern of phenomena that I am investigating,' he spoke as if from a script.

'Don't you even say hello?' my mother asked, face in shade under the brim of the hat.

He smiled. 'I'm sorry, Mrs Rothwell. This will all be handled very sensitively. I am not here to make a name for myself. I am a man of science, a psychiatrist. I do not wish to stir up trouble of any kind, just to find out what is going on and what it means. I am interested only in the truth.'

Mr Bowen frowned and bent down to pick up a small pebble from the ground, the cat wandered to his chair and sat at his feet.

'You can talk to Natasha,' my mother said.

Dr Black looked surprised at the ease with which she had agreed and he removed his hat. There was the faint jingle of the ice-cream van on the seafront. Mr Bowen sat back in his chair and looked up to the sky. I wondered why she had changed her mind.

'But we do not want publicity of any kind, she is not doing interviews with that journalist or anyone else, she must only speak to you and it must be here,' she said, gesturing to the house.

Dr Black nodded slowly. 'Thank you. It is important to listen to her.' He briefly flicked his eyes in my direction

'Natasha has spoken of her dreams since she was very young. I thought it was just an acute awareness of things, a sensitivity,' she said faintly.

Dr Black looked at her and for a second he was just like all the others, a heat in his eyes and a desire to capture or restrain her in some way.

'When she was six she was watering the flowers and she turned to me and said there'd been an accident. I didn't know what she was talking about but she insisted a man had fallen. I asked where and she didn't know, except that there was water nearby.' My mother sounded lost in the memory of the afternoon.

'I stayed with her all night, in case she had the dream again. But she slept peacefully and I thought no more of it. . . until the next evening, when we heard that a man out walking the Ridge had not returned. A search party went out and he was found at the bottom of the cliffs, in the water,' she finished.

I held my breath as she spoke. I remembered nothing of this incident. I had broken my vow of silence more than once, apparently.

Dr Black touched her arm and she didn't recoil but looked down at his hand, like it was something strange and alien. They stayed motionless for a moment as if in a dream themselves, the air singing around them. Mr Bowen stood up suddenly, he seemed to expand himself, and walked slowly to my mother's side. She turned to look at him, and smiled gently.

'It is consciousness, not matter, that connects us,' Dr Black said. '*Let me show you alive a world where every particle of dust breathes forth its joy.*'

As he spoke the words I could smell the earth on the Ridge that last night with Marcus, sense the throb in the ground below and his mouth close to mine. Everything was alive.

'You have written a book, about your work?' Mr Bowen asked, shading his eyes.

'Yes,' said Dr Black, dragging his gaze from me.

'Can you give us a copy? So we can better understand your methods.'

'I will have it delivered to you.' Dr Black began to walk backwards to the gate. 'It's charming here.' He pointed to the house and the garden. 'I look forward to our talks, Natasha,' he said.

'Yes,' I answered, nodding.

'They are planning vigils on the beach.' He put his hat back on.

Mr Bowen looked off down the coast.

'Why?' I called out.

'Fear,' he answered, looking at me intently. Then shrugging his shoulders, 'And wonder.'

As he disappeared down the steps, my mother walked over to me quickly and took me in her arms. She was shaking slightly and I held her tight. She felt clammy and hot and the straw of her hat scratched my cheek. I was happy that she had remembered at least one of my dreams and that not everything about me had been locked away in her silence.

'I thought you didn't believe me,' I said.

'I always believed you, that's why I'm afraid.'

Mr Bowen looked left out, uncomfortable, and wandered into the orchard, the cat like a shadow at his feet.

The Beauty of Impossible Things

'It wasn't a contest between you and Mr Bowen,' my therapist says, her chin in her hand.

'It was in a way.'

Chapter Thirteen

As July wore on it became quite commonplace to say that there was something evil on the Ridge. A boy was reported to have been chased by a shadowy figure in the bushes. All the kids were talking about it and trying to find out who the boy was, even some of the traders in town started to believe, whispering it to the tourists they knew and liked – don't let the kids off on their own in the trees. The lights were only the beginning, a signal that something or someone malevolent was playing with us all from up high on their perch above the town.

Marcus was at the centre of the debate. When he wasn't working in the shop he could be found on the beach, a large group of boys around him, drinking and discussing various theories. They were going to camp out, light a fire and stay up there all night, on the lookout. They were loud, pumped up and filled with a furtive bravado. He never seemed to be alone any more, a crowd of boys always within his vicinity – throwing him a ball, sharing chips or just pushing him off walls. When I caught sight of him in the distance, I thought how he looked different from them, not less well off but stronger, leaner and older too. He seemed to be playing with them as if it were a kind of joke or he was testing out a version of himself. He had a natural authority that allowed him to be with them, but not exactly be one of them. I think this was what the girls saw in him too; he had enough distance from the group to be someone they could talk to, a sense that he was his own person. He didn't need anyone's approval, or so I kept thinking, until I couldn't any more.

'Are the lights coming back?' he would ask when we'd meet.

Our friendship reduced to a transaction about black arts somehow.

'Yes,' I said.

The heat was building and added to the strange, stifling mood of the town. Some of the metal tracks on the train lines had melted and the station had to close; a stream of buses daily deposited new travellers near the bandstand. They would emerge blinking into the white glare, laden down with suitcases and beachballs. And the nights were unbearable, my bedroom like a furnace, the long windows thrown open to moonlight, moths and thoughts of Marcus. My companions in sleeplessness.

I ran into Mike Ryan on one of these days on the seafront on my bike.

'You will let me know. . . your talks with Black, or anything you hear that is happening, keep me in the loop,' he said, pushing his cap back. There was a conspiratorial tone to his words which seemed vaguely ridiculous.

'There are going to be other people wanting to talk to you.' He nodded his head.

As I cycled home some of the older boys who hung out at Barclay's Garage were sitting on the steps of the bandstand. They went silent as I cycled past, but then one of them threw a stick at my wheels, the bike came to an abrupt halt and I almost went over the handlebars.

'You seen any ghosts lately?' someone shouted.

'Hey, have you had any dreams about me?' another called.

* * *

A few days later Lewis was beaten up, he had been found cut and bruised on the path to the Ridge. This time his mother had gone to the guards to make a complaint though he did not seem to be able to describe who had done it. I called to see him but he refused to tell me anything – he seemed more withdrawn and anxious than usual and when I suggested we go and see my mother for lemonade, he shook his head. I was about to leave when he grabbed my hand tightly but his face was turned away, his neck white and contorted in shape. It was the first and last time we ever touched.

Marcus knew who had hurt him but wouldn't tell me. We were sunbathing the next morning on the rocks, the cool green water lapping and making our submerged feet look white and unearthly. We hadn't hung out for a few days, he never seemed to be alone any more.

'We need to protect Lewis,' I said, shading my eyes from the sun.

Marcus slipped off the rocks and into the sea.

'Nice,' he said, smiling.

'Don't you care?' I asked.

He shrugged his shoulders. 'Come in. . .' he replied.

I heard Victoria's voice in my head again telling me about the other girl, the one who went to the cave, and felt a prickly sense of irritation with him. I knew it was she who was responsible for the new energy in him, a lightness and not-caring air to his being, like everything was a joke.

'Don't you mind about Lewis?' I asked again.

'Not that much, he's not my problem really,' he said, turning and swimming out from the rocks.

I picked up some shells and threw them at his back. His shoulders, broad and strong, emerged from the water as he waded back to the rocks, wiping his face.

'Everything is changed now, you know that, there are no rules,' he said, leaning back against the rocks.

His blue eyes looked turquoise, his arms were pink and covered in droplets of seawater. He was taking deep breaths, his chest rising and falling. 'We can say and do what we want and you are queen of it all.' He whistled as he spoke the words.

'Maybe I don't want to be queen, that's not what it's about at all.' I replied, kicking the water.

'Isn't it?' He turned to look up at me.

'Lewis got beaten up,' I said. 'At least pretend to care, for my sake.'

'Lewis spends all night on the Ridge,' he added. 'He talks to the sky. . .'

'Isn't that what we're doing?'

He spat out an arc of water. A speedboat went past in the middle distance, we watched it flash by and travel up the coast.

'Lewis spies on people. The couples who fuck there,' he said.

He enjoyed saying the word 'fuck' to me. Perhaps he watched them too now.

'And for all we know he's the one who chased that kid. Maybe it's him up there with a blue torch,' he said.

I could hear the words of the others in his voice. 'Lewis would be scared of the child, not the other way round,' I answered.

'Come in here. . .' he said then, pointing to the water and pulling my arm.

I shook my head. He knew I was afraid of water.

'I'll teach you to swim. It can be our secret,' he said, smiling.

'We're having dinner.' I looked down the beach to the cliffs.

'You need to lighten up – being a prophet and all that must be tiring,' he said, sighing and leaning back on the rocks again.

'What is your problem?' I was trying to get to my feet. The rocks were slippery and sharp at the same time.

'Victoria saw Mr Bowen kissing your mother,' he called after me.

A day returned, from long ago. I was digging a hole in the sand. I was going to dig further and deeper than ever before. My mother was wearing a sun hat and staring out to sea. I kept trying to get her attention but she didn't move her gaze from the horizon.

'That's not true,' I said, turning back.

'Why would she lie?' His white arm was stretched out on the rocks at my feet.

It would be pointless to explain to him why girls lied about each other. I felt exhausted in his presence now, something I had never felt before.

'When did she say this?' I asked, sitting back down beside him.

'Yesterday, but she said it was a few days ago, she saw them in town.' And then he added, 'Holding hands when they walked too.'

'My mother would absolutely never do that, she hates people knowing anything about us. It's just gossip as usual.' I picked up a pebble and threw it in the water.

Marcus leaned his head back to the sun again and laughed. 'That's ironic. Everyone talks about you.' Then, biting his lip, 'I heard a drunk once talk about what he would like to do with your mother. It was in the shop one night.'

'Don't,' I said, feeling sick. 'Do you like that girl from the beach?' I knew he was thinking about her.

He looked away. 'She's all right,' he answered, knowing immediately who I spoke about.

The swiftness of his response only added to my suspicions. 'Why do you like her?' I asked.

I could see them on the Ridge together and he was touching her, his mouth resting in worship on her chest. I started to cough and used the towel to cover my splutters.

'I'm not talking about that,' he said.

'Why not? You talk to other people about it,' I replied.

'Because it's nothing to do with you,' he answered sharply. He was uncomfortable. He reached for his towel and buried his face in it, then started to dry his hair. 'I don't like anyone, OK?'

I stared out to sea. 'I never really see you,' I said.

'You're too busy preaching on the prom.'

'No, I'm not, I'm too scared to do that again,' I answered.

He smiled then and put his arm around me, pulling me close to his neck. He squeezed me tight like I was an errant little sister.

'You are the one pushing me away, meeting Black on your own,' he said suddenly.

I turned to look up at him – there were droplets of seawater on his chin, they looked delicate, like teardrops. 'That's not true, you can meet him any time,' I answered, pulling away from his arm.

'We were in this together and now it's all about you,' he said, shaking his head slightly and reaching down to touch the wet rocks.

'We are in it together, you're the one who acted weird and afraid on the Ridge that last time.'

'Fuck you.' He stood up quickly, grabbing his towel.

It was as if I had scalded him. I nearly overbalanced into the water.

'Well, you did actually, you didn't come into the trees with me. I said.

'Mike Ryan thinks you had your dream about the town flooding before the lights, but it was after, days after,' he stood tall above me.

'What?' I squinted into the sun, trying to see his face properly.

'Everyone thinks it was the other way round.'

'You told Mike my dream was before we saw the lights,' I answered, getting up. 'I never said that.'

'Did I?' He had turned away and was looking down the beach.

'I never make things up. You know that.'

'Well, is it the end of the world? Is something bad going to happen?' he shouted.

'I think so.'

'They all think you're creepy, as fucking weird as Lewis, do you know that?' He spat the words out.

'I don't care. I'm not looking to be popular, I just want to understand the lights and save people.'

'Save people! What are you, some kind of a superhero? And you hate people, you hate everyone.'

'I don't hate everyone.'

'You just want everyone to admire you, the thought of being ordinary is what you hate, that's why you are telling people this stuff and. . .' He had stopped himself before too much came out.

'Do you think I'm ordinary?'

'Look, I have to go,' he said, starting to walk away.

'Marcus!' I called after him.

But he didn't turn back.

Chapter Fourteen

After our argument I kept away from town for the the rest of that week and little news or gossip reached our door. Marcus called a few times over those days but I refused to see him. Victoria came once, too. I watched from my window as they talked and laughed on their way back to the gate, Marcus giddy and grabbing her sunglasses.

Mr Bowen meanwhile stepped up his attentions with my mother, or maybe after what Marcus said I just noticed it more. Our home was filled with a new kind of silence, one that was no longer distracted but charged instead with an anticipation of some kind that became deeper and more mysterious as the day gave way. There was a new and unfamiliar tone around the house, the air of idleness replaced with something much more alive and real, desire I suppose. It was like a wakeful beast stalking the hot, airless rooms. I became the guest, an uninvited one.

Dinner was invariably late. My mother bathed in the early evenings, incense and steam wafting down the stairs. Her face flushed, hair still wet at the dinner table, a fresh dress on and a wine glass in her hand. After dinner, they would leave for the garden where she would read on a blanket at the edge of the orchard, he lying beside her, his legs outstretched, arms under his head, staring at the evening sky. Occasionally he offered her pages of his manuscript to read, the cat asleep beside them. She would take them from him as if they were a precious gift bestowed, the secrets of his being contained in the neat sentences. They would talk softly into the night, the light fading and the garden growing dark all around them. I would close the curtains then.

I wondered for a time if her interest in him was just a way to escape having to think about me. She could share her fears and worries with him and he would rationally explain them all away. She could forget for a time that I was embroiled in a strange tale overtaking the town. This was only partly true, though, I was not the centre of their story.

I watched them endlessly, determined to never leave them alone. I hounded them with my gaze, every glance and every move they made subject to silent interpretation. My mother's requests for me to go into town and collect something were met with a blank refusal; Mr Bowen would check his shadow, only to find me there.

I woke most nights that week to wild electrical storms in the dark sky, the air in my room heavy, stifling and dry; the unlocked French doors of the dining room below loosened and free, banging against the side of the house. My mother and sometimes Mr Bowen with her, creeping down the stairs to try and secure them. Once I saw them walk together in the garden at midnight, the sky alight over the Ridge with flashes of lightning, he leading her away from the gravel path and into the swaying darkness of the apple trees.

My dreams about Mr Bowen started in those few days of isolation in the house at the end of July and they added to the air of destruction I felt all around me. In one the pages of his manuscript were raining down from the trees in the orchard like a strange snow; in another he was lying bleached white on the beach, a light grey sky above and the sea rising and beside him was Lewis, turned on his side, inert and facing the Ridge, his clothes sopping wet. I woke with the feel of sand and water in my mouth.

I monitored Mr Bowen with new eyes after the dreams began; his fate, as well as his desire for my mother, were questions to be considered more deeply. He worked most mornings at the desk in his room. He would be writing, papers everywhere, his graceful neck, lean, tanned and strong, bent over his work. His pen furious some mornings, idle the next as he stared at the wall in front of him. A few clothes would be strewn across the bed, a painting of my mother's propped against the wall and the window open, the long thin curtain blowing gently inwards in the breeze. He would turn suddenly when he sensed me there at the door, a faint look of surprise on his face that he then tried to hide. He would gesture for me to enter but I declined his invitation every time. There was nothing to say, each of us an interruption to the other.

I never felt he hated or really disliked me, even then I understood that. We were a puzzle to each other, he was using all the powers of his rational mind to try and work out what I was about, while I dragged the unconscious looking for signs and symbols as to the meaning of him. I lay awake in my narrow bed wondering why they had to meet and what it meant, my belief in a determined world ensuring I never saw anything as random. He had come for a reason, like the strange lights in the sky, and the girl who went into caves.

Many years later I took my mother's paintings out of storage and wept over them. I pitied her efforts yet loved her more for their imperfections. I recognized my face in almost all of the people she had drawn – a dark insolent stare peering back at me, the eyes knowing but cold, a distance in them. The strange figure in the picture that she kept trying to capture over and over was me, and I had never been able to see that before. All the stories she had inside her were distorted and reduced to this one unforgiving and dominant image. I told my therapist there was not a single sketch of Mr Bowen. And for a long time I fooled myself into thinking the absence of his face in her drawings meant she had never really loved him.

'I forgive him now,' I tell my therapist.

'Forgive him?' she asks.

'For loving her,' I explain.

* * *

Dr Black returned towards the end of that lost week. We sat in the study. He rested his cream hat on the mahogany desk, touching the surface of the wood briefly before laying it down. For a minute he didn't speak – his head was tilted slightly, watching me.

'You know I help people who feel different, who are confused, worried about things,' he said, his brown eyes large and bright. 'I especially listen to teenagers and children who believe they have experienced something out of the ordinary, I try and understand this experience. . .

'Tell me something of yourself,' he said.

'I don't have a father, he left. We live alone, except when the guests come in the summer,' I answered.

The words came out without me thinking, I wasn't sure they were relevant. There was surely more to me than this.

'I am sorry about that,' Dr Black answered softly.

He loosened his tie slightly and closed his eyes briefly.

'And I dream things, then they happen,' I said.

'What have your dreams been about this week?' he asked.

'Mr Bowen mostly, the man staying here, and Lewis, my friend, sometimes.'

We didn't speak for a few seconds. I fiddled with the cushion.

'I dream about Mr Bowen dying, drowning and some other

things,' I explained.

An image came to me of his head bowed in front of my mother, the room red with their desire.

'Have you spoken to your mother about your feelings towards Mr Bowen?' he asked.

I shook my head.

'Change is unsettling and can trigger things. . .' he replied.

'I felt it the day he arrived at the house. There was bad luck in the air, all around him.'

'Your anxiety about what has been happening – the lights may be manifesting in fear around him, a new man living here.'

'He doesn't live here, he's just staying for a while.'

He nodded. 'And who is Lewis?' he asked.

'A friend, he saw the lights too.'

'I would like to speak with him also, perhaps you can arrange it?' he asked.

'He won't talk to you, he doesn't like strangers.'

Dr Black sighed deeply and reached up to touch some of the books.

'I was travelling recently in South America,' he said.

'What were you doing there?' I asked, standing beside him.

'I went to meet and interview some school students, they believed they had been visited by aliens.' He looked down at me briefly.

His words were permanent, heavy, like an obstacle that landed in the path ahead of you, blocking your easy route. You had a choice whether to go back, or go over.

'Did you believe them?' I asked.

'I believed they told me the truth, as far as they knew it to be the truth,' he said, turning and leaning against the bookshelves.

'Might they have been mad?' I asked.

'I saw signs of trauma, but not mental instability. This is what I have come to recognize – perfectly sane people sometimes have extraordinary experiences that are almost impossible for science to explain. Do you believe you are mad?' His eyebrows were raised.

'No, not at all.'

'What did you feel that last night on the Ridge?' he asked, walking over to the window.

'I felt a presence.'

'A fearful thing. . .?'

'No, if anything it was beautiful. I felt connected, I felt it deep in the earth, like a throb from below that then emerged into lights. It's hard to explain.'

'I see.' He nodded, his eyes serious now. 'And you felt it had a message?'

'Yes, about death,' I said.

'That is grave.'

I looked up at him and he was smiling. 'It's not a joke,' I snapped.

'Of course not. Does it frighten you – the precognition?'

'What do you mean, precognition?' I asked.

'The ability to see things ahead of time, predict them?'

'I know nothing else, so no – but I didn't predict the lights, it's other things but not the lights. I didn't expect them. I had dreams about them afterwards though.'

'That is not overly important right now. You witnessed them,' he said.

'I just wanted to tell you that I hadn't predicted them.'

'Are you ashamed, guilty at not having dreamed about them in advance?' he asked, eyebrows raised again.

'No.' I felt my face go red.

'I'm glad. I only ask because it seems you have been hiding out this week and I wondered if it was fear or shame keeping you away.'

'I needed time, to think about how I tell more people, explain to them.'

He nodded. 'It takes bravery, courage to show people who you are. There is a responsibility to it. I very much admired your speech on the promenade the other week.'

'It's the very thing my mother hates. She doesn't want people to know who I am, not that I told her I spoke to the crowd. She would ground me completely if she knew – speaking at the meeting in the hotel was bad enough.'

'She is naturally protective. People will make judgements, they will want to prove you wrong,' he said. 'She is right about that and remember she has allowed us to meet which is something.'

I went and stood beside him. The apple trees in the orchard outside the window were heavy with fruit and filled with butterflies; long shadows crept over the grass.

'It has changed out there, you should know that,' he said, pointing in the direction of the town.

'How?' I asked.

'People are afraid and they behave in ways they would not normally and that is why I am here, to protect you.' He was looking at me sideways.

'Do you have children?' I asked.

He bowed his head briefly and moved away from the window back to the desk. 'Another day, we can talk about that,' he said.

'The children... the ones in South America, what happened to them?' I sensed he was ready to leave and wanted to delay him.

'They were shunned, disbelieved,' he said quietly.

'I followed the lights into the trees,' I said suddenly.

'And what did you find?' he asked, a tightness or urgency behind the words.

'They were leading me somewhere, but I didn't want to go yet.'

'Why not?'

'I might not come back.'

'I see,' he answered.

We stood in silence for a moment.

'Where might the somewhere they were leading you be?' he asked. 'If everything is coming to an end.'

'I don't know, it just felt like it might be safe to follow them, to believe in them, I think they are spirits of the dead,' I said.

He put his hand to his mouth and for a second he looked completely exhausted, old and withered. I wondered had I said the wrong thing and perhaps he only knew about aliens. I picked up the journal I kept of my dreams from the desk and gave it to him. It looked embarrassing, bits of glitter stuck to it.

'You can read them, it's my dreams, other things that I saw that did come true,' I said.

He looked down at the notebook. 'I'm not here to test you.'

'Aren't you?' I asked.

'I would hate for you to think that,' he replied, a crease between his eyes.

'Everyone is here to test everyone else, I think.'

Chapter Fifteen

When Dr Black left, I went out to the garden. It was after six and the intense heat was subsiding. My mother had laid out a picnic on a blanket; Mr Bowen wandered out after a while, a bottle of wine under his arm along with the newspaper.

'I might go to the beach tonight.' I picked at some bread.

'You should – you've been in all week, Marcus keeps calling,' she said, laying more food out.

Mr Bowen sat down cross-legged opposite me and opened the paper.

'You look like you'd prefer a chair,' I said.

He tilted his head back and laughed. My mother was still unpacking food but stopped and watched him, her cheeks flushed briefly. She looked proud of him, as if she could not quite believe he was really there.

'You have me well understood,' he replied, staring at me.

My mother handed me some lemonade.

'How did it go with Black?' he asked.

'He's a very interesting man, he thinks I have precognition.'

'Oh, I see.' My mother frowned and pretended to know what it meant. She should have been more interested really, she was always on the verge of noticing my life, but then would drift away.

'And how does that work with the rules of physics?' Mr Bowen said.

'What do you mean?' I asked.

'Cause and effect.' He looked away from me to my mother.

'He is a doctor,' she answered thoughtfully.

'I don't doubt it.' He bit into a sandwich and looked out to the coast.

* * *

The seafront seemed unusually crowded that night and I was nervous to be out of the cocoon of the house. The sky was orange and pink over the horizon, the sea calm, a lone yacht far in the distance, and there was another fire on the Ridge, a spiral of smoke drifting out to the coast. Some boys flew past on bikes, while kids were calling out high above the sand, strapped onto the arm of the big dipper, legs dangling over the sea. Councillor Barry and his henchmen were standing in an uneasy huddle of smoke outside Marcus's shop.

Things had changed, Dr Black was right. The warm evening air seethed with an excited, suspicious unease; people moved along the seafront quickly, their lethargy forgotten, everyone going somewhere, expecting something. They had been released from the stifling heat of the day into a cooler night where almost anything might be possible, the bars along the shoreline providing an energetic, muffled soundtrack to their mood. There was a sense that something unusual and out of the ordinary was taking place, and we were all part of the show.

I went down the steps to the beach. Some families were on blankets, picnic baskets open and binoculars lying in the sand. A group of people all dressed in white were doing exercise. They bent and swayed in unison, while chanting. The owner of the caravan park, Jim, sat on a blanket watching them and he waved to me as I passed. There was a crowd in a semicircle near the end of the beach at the foot of the Ridge, some vans selling burgers parked up beside them.

I threaded in and out of people – a couple played frisbee; an old woman was on her knees praying, head down; a group of men had set up telescopes and were pointing at the sky. I saw a bright white light on black stilts – a TV crew were setting up. A woman in a fancy yellow dress held a microphone, a few men around her lined up a camera and took equipment out of large silver boxes that looked like shiny, washed-up treasure chests.

I recognized the wonder Dr Black had spoken about. I walked to the edge of the shore, the sand dissolving and subsiding under my feet, and turned from the sea to the crowd. The Ridge loomed purple and gold behind them, the sky above empty. I had to speak to them, reach out, tell them they were right to be here on the beach at twilight, right to believe that something bigger, darker was above us in the heavens. We were right to be afraid; the lights were a warning that nothing was impossible.

'If you are not afraid, you have not been paying attention,' I shouted.

At first no one listened, they barely noticed another body in the throng of people.

'We are not alone any more,' I called out.

A few stopped what they were doing and began to gather closer.

'They have come to tell us about the end,' I said.

'Who has?' a man shouted.

I noticed Lewis then, he was sitting right on the edge of the water, where the sand was wet, white foam reaching ever closer to him. Some people laughed and a can was thrown, a few moved away but others stayed, their faces serious in the evening light.

'What can we do?' one asked.

'Wait,' I replied.

They nodded and some looked back up to the Ridge looming large behind them.

'And see what they ask of us.'

There was shouting on the promenade and the burst of an exhaust like gunfire. People turned and slowly began to drift away. They were like waves, drawing closer and then away from me again. I kept trying to catch them and never quite did.

I crouched down beside Lewis who had come beside me; his breathing was heavy, his skin white and waxy. There was a cut above his eye and his tongue protruded slightly from his mouth. He didn't look at me but slowly traced the shape of a giant eye in the sand. There was another loud bang and Lewis jumped. His eyes met mine in a flash of fear.

'It's nothing, just a motorbike,' I said, pointing to the path that led to the Ridge where its red tail light was flashing.

He pointed to the drawing in the sand and then to the navy sky.

'I know,' I said, nodding my head.

He stared at me then, something he never usually did, and his eyes were not vacant but alert and awake.

'They're coming again,' I whispered.

'Cyclops,' he said softly, quietly. His words were as clear as anything, like before he broke down, when people had thought he might be a genius. 'They watch me,' he said, leaning close.

I traced the outline of the drawing with my finger; he put his hand out to touch mine, and then pulled it back. 'Third eye.' He pointed to my forehead.

'They are not Cyclops, Lewis, it's something else.' I looked up, the crowd kept moving, wandering past, their heads raised to the darkening sky over the Ridge.

He pointed again to my forehead.

'Ms Rothwell. . .' shouted a voice from behind us.

I looked up to see Councillor Barry.

'Be careful, you have to be careful.' I whispered to Lewis.

He was walking quickly towards us, a megaphone in his hand. I could feel Lewis tighten and shrink inside himself.

'Look at this. . .' Councillor Barry said, gesturing along the beach. 'You have to put a stop to it, it's dangerous, it's getting out of control.'

'Stop what?' I asked.

'Preaching, stirring rumours – you and that Black man,' he said. 'Look.' He pointed along the crowded beach again. 'You need to come with me.' He took my arm suddenly and it hurt, like a Chinese burn.

Lewis jumped to his feet, put his hands over his ears and emitted a piercing scream.

'For God's sake,' said Councillor Barry, trying to hang on to me.

I struggled to free myself from his grasp and kicked out at him. Lewis kicked too, the eye in the sand dissolved under our feet and he ran away towards the Ridge. 'Don't,' I called after Lewis.

But he didn't turn back and disappeared into the crowd.

'Natasha, Natasha,' Mr Bowen shouted. He had emerged from the water, a towel around his shoulders, and was jogging towards us.

Councillor Barry dropped my arm.

'Don't touch her. . .' Mr Bowen was out of breath.

'She's a bloody nuisance, look at this, look at it. . .' Councillor Barry answered. 'Lights, what bloody lights, no one but a few drunks and this one here have seen them,' he shouted at Mr Bowen and then glanced angrily down at me.

'That is not true,' I said, looking from one to the other.

'Well, the town is busy, that should make you happy,' Mr Bowen said to him, taking my hand gently and walking me away from the water's edge.

'Let's just get home,' he said under his breath.

'The lights aren't coming tonight, Councillor Barry, if you want to tell them that,' I shouted back, pointing at the megaphone.

'Leave it,' Mr Bowen said.

His hand was soft, light in mine, different to Marcus's grip which was always so tight.

'This is getting crazy,' he said, looking at me sideways as we walked. His hair was wet and black, clinging to the side of his tanned face, sand on his lean arms. I let his hand go.

'How are you sure the lights aren't coming?' he asked.

'I just know, it's not tonight,' I replied.

'What do you think they are?' he asked hesitantly.

'I don't know, maybe it's God,' I answered.

'I didn't think you were religious.'

'I'm not.'

He smiled briefly to himself. A young woman in a short

dress stumbled across our path. She was carrying a bottle of beer and smiled at Mr Bowen.

'And your mother?' he asked.

'She believes in nothing but art and flowers, and sometimes communism,' I said.

He laughed.

'But I'm sure you already know that.'

'I don't know much really.' He looked away to the sea.

We walked on, weaving silently through bodies that were staring up at the sky.

'There is nothing wrong with believing in something, in thinking differently about it compared to your mother,' he said.

'I know,' I answered. 'We are not the same people. She is far more romantic than me.'

He looked at me briefly again as we walked.

'Perhaps that will come with time. Have you spoken to Black about your mother, your life here?'

'No, not yet, we've only just started talking and it's not about that anyway, it's about the lights, my dreams.'

'You know if it ever doesn't feel comfortable with him. . .'

'The lights have come for a reason,' I replied. 'We don't fully know why yet, but they are here and it's my job to help people believe, to understand.'

He didn't immediately answer but looked out past me again to the sea. 'That's a burden to carry,' he finally said.

'It's what I was born for. I'm not like other people.'

'You should talk about that with him, but maybe also about your life with your mother. I know maybe it has been hard, growing up here.'

I've come to believe he understood us more completely than anyone else really, even though his time in our company was short.

'We have a very good life here and I'm very happy,' I snapped back.

We were nearing the bandstand end of the beach when I saw Marcus. He was talking to the cave girl and he looked excited, his hands were flying, so I knew he was describing something to her. She appeared less interested. He didn't notice me in the crowds. She leaned her head against the side of the bandstand and he did too. His gestures were so familiar to me but tonight they were different, they were being put to another, alien use in which I played no part. He existed separate to me, in his own world.

A group of men pushed past and I stumbled into the sand. It was mesmerizing to watch him with her, and despite the dread I felt, there was a part of me that wanted to stay, to watch him touch her and understand how it would make him feel.

'Are you all right?' Mr Bowen offered his hand which I didn't take.

'Do you think I'm beautiful?' I looked up at him.

He flushed red and crossed his arms. 'I don't think it's right or appropriate that I answer that,' he replied.

'It's just a fact, and you like facts. My mother is beautiful, isn't she?' I said, kneeling.

People brushed past us, and sand flicked up at my face. I could feel the grit in my hair, smell the sea on my skin. He looked out to the horizon and I felt the sadness again, the overwhelming sense of him bowed under something dark and hopeless.

'She is very beautiful,' he answered.

'And it's why you came here. . .'

He looked down at me and his face was pained. He held out his hand again, but once more I refused. I got to my feet and we crossed the road to the gate in silence. The steps to the house loomed tall. He walked slowly ahead of me, into the dusky light, pushing back the overgrown forsythia bushes and clearing a way for me. When we got to the top, I tripped over the final step and fell on to the grass. He turned suddenly and picked me up in a rush, nearly unbalancing before steadying himself and carrying me slowly along the gravel path to the front door. His breaths were deep, his gaze fixed on the house and the long, lit windows. I could make out the stubble of his beard and he smelled of salt and the sea, his brown skin still damp.

'I can get down,' I said, embarrassed.

'Do you feel dizzy? I'll get you a cold drink. This day's heat is draining everyone, it can hit you anytime.' His brow furrowed.

I shook my head and he left me standing on the front step and moved to push open the door. There was a faint echo of music from the back of the house, the record player on, my mother waiting for him to return from his swim.

'There is shadow, a darkness, over you,' I said, and the words floated between us in the still night air.

He stopped completely still, looking ahead at the door, his hand flat against it, veins twisting in the side of his neck as he swallowed.

'I saw it in a dream. Lewis was there too, both of you lying on the beach.'

I tell my therapist I have thought about this moment often. When I re-imagine it, everything works out differently. He doesn't stay silent but gets angry instead, slams his fist against the door, calls my mother out into the twilight, and she makes me explain myself. I tell him then that he must be careful, the fates are awake to him; he listens intently and packs his things.

'And you believed it truly? That he was in danger?' She leans forward in her seat.

'Yes,' I reply.

'And what did he do when you spoke so?'

'Nothing. He just opened the door and went in search of my mother.'

Chapter Sixteen

Marcus was outside his shop the next morning, sluicing the front steps with a bucket of water. It was sunny but not as warm, a light easterly breeze had kicked a hole in the heat.

'I need to see you later,' I said, cycling up to him.

He jumped in surprise, then was embarrassed, shuffling his feet; his hair covered his tired eyes and he smelled vaguely of beer. It felt deeply awkward to stand in front of him, something it never had before.

'Lewis is missing,' he said.

'But I saw him last night, what do you mean?' Panic rose in my chest.

'He didn't come home, the Guards called here looking for him earlier,' he replied, glancing to the Ridge.

'But I was with him and then he ran, he ran away towards the Ridge,' I said. I had been distracted with Councillor Barry and Mr Bowen, how could I have let him run like that? Guilt flowed through me.

'When?'

'On the beach, about nine or so, he got a fright and then he just ran.'

My throat seemed to be closing over, it was difficult to swallow and I felt a throbbing pain over my left eye.

'I saw him around then too,' Marcus said, his cheeks flushed, eyes darting.

'After that girl dumped you?'

He looked embarrassed again and rubbed his hair. 'I don't know who you mean, and where have you been anyway? I called over.'

'At home. . . thinking,' I answered. Then, 'Are we still friends?' I asked.

He looked startled and gazed past me to the beach. 'Yes, I mean. . .' he said, looking down.

I have often wondered what that 'I mean' really meant, and where it was leading to and I regret that I didn't ask him to finish that sentence. I might have understood things so much more clearly if I had done so.

'Everyone is talking about you, the fact that you weren't around,' he said.

'Who?' I asked.

'The kids on the beach, some other people too, Victoria.'

I noticed he had a small silver stud in his ear. 'When did you get that done?' I asked, reaching up to touch it.

'With some people, up near the casino, a few days ago.' He shifted slightly away from me. 'They're doing tattoos there too, not real ones though, they come off,' he said, looking over my shoulder to the sea. 'I think I'll get a real one, maybe in the city.'

The conversation seemed empty, pointless and unfamiliar.

'Perhaps Lewis just camped out, though it isn't like him. I'll have to tell Mum, she'll want us to help.' I looked away to the Ridge again. 'He'll be so afraid if he is on his own or hurt up there.'

Marcus didn't answer but looked down at the bucket which was vibrating in his shaking hand, water spilling onto the ground.

'I mean, it can't be, he can't go missing, he must be hiding. We need to search now,' I said.

He gestured back to the shop. 'I can't, I'm working.'

His mother was visible in the window, cleaning down the counters.

'Do you know something about last night? Did anyone try and scare him, beat him up again?' I asked.

I moved the bike forward slightly, and it almost ran over his foot.

'Watch out.' He stepped back and gave me a sullen stare. 'I don't know anything about what happened to Lewis last night. I was busy with something else.' And he walked back into his shop.

* * *

'It's so awful, I can't think straight,' my mother said.

She was putting dishes away in the kitchen later that afternoon. There had been no news yet as to Lewis's whereabouts. She kept pacing up and down, starting tasks and then not finishing them. She had also rung his mother and the guards several times to try and find out information, but no one knew anything yet.

'I'm going to help in the search this afternoon,' she said.

'Nobody is taking it too seriously yet, but they should. He never runs away and I've. . .' I said, stopping.

'Please finish,' she said, eyebrows raised.

'I've had some dreams about him and I tried to warn him not to go to the Ridge.'

She leaned on the table for a second, her head down. 'I painted his parents once.' She looked out the window then.

I turned to look out too. Mr Bowen was reading in the shade, sunglasses on, a pen in his hand and a sheaf of paper on the ground beside him. We had not spoken since the evening before.

'When?' I asked.

'Years ago, before he was born. I called it *The Wedding Party*. They were on the bandstand having their photos taken and she was wearing a blue wedding dress, all frills and a veil. It was the most extraordinary sight, she was trying to hide her pregnant stomach under the bouquet. His father was smoking, restless. It was odd and not joyous in any way, to be honest.

They looked miserable together, which in the end they were.' She stood up and walked to the cupboard.

'Why a blue dress?' I asked.

'I don't know, for shame maybe, she felt she couldn't wear white,' she said, looking at me, her eyes sad.

'And she was pregnant with Lewis?' I replied.

She nodded. 'I hate weddings really, always have.' She took a vase out of one of the cupboards.

'Always?' I asked.

'Always, even as a teenager which I was when I painted that picture. I never saw the romance of it,' she said, looking at me, her gaze steady.

'Why?'

'*I shouldn't mind being a bride at a wedding. . .*' she said.

'*. . .if I could be one without having a husband,*' I finished it for her. 'Maybe whether you are wanted or not as a baby changes your life, like decides it.'

She didn't answer but gathered up the lavender she had collected and left on the table.

'Don't think everything about us was a mistake,' she said, putting them into a vase.

'Did you want me?' I asked.

'How can you even ask that? Of course I did,' she replied softly. 'I've had the life I chose.' She touched the top of my head with her gentle mouth.

I wanted to believe her, to think that our aloof existence here was all part of her life plan. Some voices from the front garden drifted in through the open windows. A woman from the city, in thin heels and a nice dress, was talking to Mr Bowen. She flicked her hair continuously and laughed gaily. She looked out of place there, all shiny and competent.

'Has Mr Bowen ever been married before?' I asked, watching them.

'No, why would you think that?' She stared at them also.

'It's just odd, isn't it, that he wouldn't have been. Women are always talking to him. I don't imagine he has to be on his own, if he doesn't want to be,' I answered, watching her.

She fiddled intently with the flowers. 'Not everyone's aim is to get married.'

'Most people do marry though.'

'Honestly, what a day to be talking of weddings, with Lewis. . .' She stopped attending to the flowers.

'I think men are far more conventional than women, don't you? Except Lewis and he is always being punished for it,' I said, feeling tears behind my eyes.

'I've never really thought about it.'

'We are told they're brave, but they aren't really, or not many of them. They don't really stand on their own.'

'Maybe they don't have to be brave, it's easier for them.' She reached out and touched my arm.

'Do you remember the day the boat went out with Lewis's dad?' I got up from the chair.

'Yes.' She looked haunted.

'Is that why you always cared for him?'

She didn't answer.

'We were guilty, we didn't help,' I said.

'We were not to know.' She sat down in the chair.

'But we did know.' I wiped my nose.

The woman outside was laughing.

'Go and see what she wants,' my mother said.

I walked through the hall and out into the front garden. The sky was clear but the air still cooler than previous days, the breeze stronger now, the trees and hedges moving and bending.

'What a delight of a place and such splendid views,' the woman was saying to Mr Bowen.

He was standing hands in his pockets looking at her, his black hair blowing gently, sunglasses still on.

'Can I help you?' I asked.

'I'm looking for a room, we're staying in town for a few days. Mike Ryan recommended you,' she said, smiling. She gave me her card, which was from a television station. Her name, *Amy Martin*, was printed on it and underneath was the word *Reporter*. I recognized her then from the beach, the lady with the TV crew.

'You'll have to call on the phone,' I said.

'Oh, I see, you can't just tell me now.'

160

I shook my head and folded my arms.

'I'll do that then.' She looked from Mr Bowen to me. 'Do you have a card?' she added.

'No,' I replied.

She looked vaguely amused as if we were quaint people. 'Can you give me your phone number then?'

My mother had come into the hall, the door open. I recited the number and the woman wrote it on her hand.

'I'll call later, thanks. . .' she said.

She smiled at Mr Bowen, and then tottered across the grass.

'You know a boy has gone missing.' She turned back from the gate.

'Yes, very worrying,' said Mr Bowen quickly.

She nodded and disappeared down the cliffs.

'She's looking for a room.' I walked back to the front door and gave my mother the card. Mr Bowen took off his sunglasses and distractedly rubbed his cheek.

'It's going to be a siege.' My mother frowned and looked over my head to him.

'They beat Lewis up last week,' I said.

'Who did?' asked Mr Bowen.

'I'm not sure, some kids. I told him last night to be careful, he was on the beach. I've been trying to warn him to stay away from the Ridge,' I answered, looking from one to the other.

My mother put her hand to her throat and retreated into the shade of the hall. Mr Bowen looked at me and there was a trace of fear in his eyes, before he quickly followed her into the house. I turned to look at the Ridge in the distance, a grey and brown mass of secrets stark against the blue of the sky.

Chapter Seventeen

I have been asked a lot of impossible questions in the years since, questions for which the answers are never straightforward; answers that have been forced to crouch, move and bend as time passes over their heads. I have come to understand that things that once made sense no longer do, an epiphany can be a passing rather than a lasting phenomenon. We are always right back at the beginning.

Dr Black talked to me about time quite a bit in the days after Lewis went missing. He called most afternoons and we would sit in the study or at the edge of the orchard. He took notes sometimes, other days not, and once he brought a tiny tape recorder that he positioned beside me as we talked. The sounds of the seafront rising and subsiding, the heat and hush of that late July forever captured on a tape somewhere along with my voice.

I have never felt as heard as I did those warm afternoons. When I look back only with regret I forget that in the midst of the sadness there was good too, that a part of me that was usually buried had a few weeks when it could emerge blinking into the sunlight. And even though this was a bad thing – for I should have kept my true self hidden away – I find that truth difficult to reconcile with the memories of the garden and the sky, his voice flowing all around me. He became a sort of father figure to me, an older man with a jaunty hat and a perspective on the world as unusual as my own.

'If time exists not as we think it does, but as something far more strange, then anything is possible. The past, the present, the future, they are one, and occasionally, if the boundaries break down, we can see things.' Dr Black was sipping his iced tea.

'So time doesn't exist?' I said, face up to the hot sun.

'Time is maybe in the absences we perceive, the gaps between memory and anticipation,' he replied.

I sat up straight in the chair, his words making a wondrous sense. The garden was filled with butterflies, the sky the deepest azure blue, the green of the trees beside us luminous and his voice mellow and rich.

'Perhaps I see the gaps,' I said.

He switched off the tape recorder and we sat in silence for a few minutes. I watched the gulls swoop and soar high above our heads. My legs stretched out before me, brown and long, my mother's only physical gift to me.

'May I ask you something?' He leaned forward.

I nodded and took a glass of lemonade off the rusted wrought-iron table between us.

'That boy Lewis, how long has he been missing now?' he asked.

'Five days,' I answered.

He shook his head and looked down at his hands. 'You mentioned before that he had seen the lights, and also that you dreamed about him, him and Mr Bowen?'

'Yes,' I replied.

'What might be the connection?'

'That they are both going to come to harm. Lewis knew, he said it to me here in the garden. I should have tried harder to protect him.' I felt tears come to my eyes and rubbed them quickly. I wanted Mr Black to see me as a rational person, just one who happened to deal in dreams.

'And Mr Bowen?' he said.

'I warned him, but he doesn't believe a single thing about me.'

'He has his reasons, I imagine, to be uncomfortable around you.' He tilted his head back into the sun.

'Yes.'

'Lewis was known to be unwell,' he said, turning to me again.

'I didn't think so, he is just unusual. Well, maybe a bit unwell.'

'He was drawn to you and your mother, I feel.'

'Yes, we like him a lot.' I thought of Lewis in the garden, my mother giving him a glass of lemonade. 'We were like another family in a way, I mean we understood him, we took the time. He fitted with us and he always tried. . . He tried to please her, he wanted to be well with us, like there was a part of him that wasn't poorly, and he kept it for us, tried to show it to us. He had a breakdown, you see, he was absolutely fine before but then everything cracked sort of,' I finished.

I briefly saw myself in the mirror, a deep gash cutting through my reflection. It was unnerving and I closed my eyes for a second.

'She seems very distressed about his disappearance,' he answered, looking out to sea then.

'She thinks I had something to do with him being on the Ridge, or the lights made him go up there, I'm not sure.'

'And did you?' His eyes were back on me.

'No, but people were making fun of him. I think they were afraid of him, like they are of me. I tried to warn him, the Ridge wasn't safe. I knew that and I should have tried harder to protect him, it's like his father all over. . .'

Dr Black handed me a handkerchief. 'His father?' he said.

'I saw him go out in his fishing boat, when I was younger, Marcus's father too, and I told my mother that they weren't going to come back but she didn't believe me and I didn't save them either,' I explained.

'You think your gift is to save other people, but perhaps that's not what it is about at all.'

It seemed an odd thing to say – what were we doing if we weren't saving people from something strange and terrible? We knew better, there was a responsibility in that.

'You save people.' I replied.

'Not really. I explore them.'

'I can't help the guilt, I said, 'it's the shadow side of seeing things, I fail all the time and. . .' I thought of my mother, her gaze averted from me.

He did not answer for a minute. Then, 'Do you think people are afraid of you?' he asked.

'When we took part in the search for Lewis, the first night on the Ridge, some people shouted at me, they said I had brought bad luck, evil to the town.' I frowned at the memory.

Men in yellow vests, dogs on leads, torches and the whispers of me, the UFO girl. My mother grabbing my hand and hurrying our descent down the hill, her red skirt trailing and snagging on branches and rocks.

'The Ridge is a bad place, people kill themselves there,' I said.

'It has been said to me before, some places prove attractive to the despairing and become associated with such things.' He nodded his head before looking to the ground. 'Do you have feelings about where Lewis might be or what has happened to him?'

I could hear my mother humming, she was weeding the lavender pots near the front door. I had been waiting to dream of him, was surprised that I hadn't yet. 'No, but I fear it isn't good.' I shook my head.

He got up and stared out to sea, his linen suit crumpled, the pattern of the chair visible on his jacket.

'Do you think I could help find him?' I asked.

'I don't know.'

A red admiral butterfly landed on the table beside me and its wings quivered before it took off again, a flash of scarlet, darting among the trees.

'Do you know what causes the brightest light in the galaxy?' he asked.

'No.'

'It's when a star dies. It emits a light that outshines everything else.' He turned back to look at me, his face in shade, serious.

'Are they the lights we are seeing on the Ridge?' I asked, confused.

He smiled sadly and looked out to the sea again. 'No, that remains a mystery,' he said. 'You know people fear the truth because it is too astonishing.'

'What truth?' I asked.

'The truth about the universe, how chaotic and utterly unpredictable it is, how the more we know, the less we understand.'

'Maybe we aren't made for chaos and change, and any change we do see coming we think will be for the better, a mind trick.' I replied.

'There is a lot in that sentence.'

'I feel their thoughts. People never give up hoping, it makes them beautiful but sad. They think the lights might bring the town money, notoriety, something that can be used, but that's not what it is about at all.'

'And your mother?' he asked, watching me.

'She doesn't think.'

'That's a harsh assessment,' he replied, eyebrows raised.

'She's worried for Lewis, suspicious of me, but mostly she is in love with Mr Bowen,' I said.

'She does believe you. It's why she hides out here. She shares your fear to some extent.'

'No, she does that because she is ashamed of herself.'

'And from where does her shame come?' he said, looking at me again.

I sat back in the chair and shaded my eyes. He was saying something no one else had ever dared. I was a shameful thing, of all the daughters she might have had. The girl she gave up everything for was not perhaps worth the effort, or the sacrifice.

'I believe your mother is key to many things, and she is not at all aware of her power,' he said.

I drank some more lemonade and looked up at the house, the peeling paint, the windows that did not shut, warped by the salt and the wind. We were not powerful people, we held the key to ephemeral dreams and nothing more.

'Do you know that on one of Saturn's icy moons there are lakes and rivers of methane, and that it rains diamonds on Neptune?' he said. He started to laugh, great, deep guffaws that caused him to hold his stomach, and the sound echoed throughout the garden. I imagined people far below on the seafront could have heard him. 'All the impossible things that are quite real.' He wiped his forehead with a handkerchief. 'Just remember that when any mock you,' he added.

'I will, I do.'

'And if you can, try and focus on Lewis and lose your sense of guilt – being able to shed light on his disappearance might help our case,' he said.

'What case?'

'The case for truth, belief. And it would make your mother happy. She might see you for the good you can bring.'

I had not thought about it that way.

'We are changing them, together, and I have great plans for us.' He folded his arms and stared at the sea. 'Let's go to the shore now,' he said, excited suddenly, his energy renewed. 'They believe in you.' He turned to look at me.

'I'm not sure they do,' I said, reluctant to leave the garden. 'I'm not good at making them listen.'

'I'll show you, come.' His hand reached out for mine.

* * *

We walked down the steps and along the promenade to the bandstand. The beach was busy, the amusements flashing, sirens and whistles blaring, while a number of police cars lined the shore. The booming sounds of a man with a megaphone could be heard at the foot of the Ridge, though his words were distorted and lost on the breeze.

'Speak.' Dr Black pointed to the centre of the bandstand.

'I don't know what to say.' I felt nervous and exposed, my mother's face in my head, and I wanted to run away, but somehow there was no turning back now. I couldn't disappoint him.

'What did he want from you?' my therapist asks now.

And I'm never really sure how to answer.

'Proof, I think,' I reply.

But it was more than that, he didn't just want my visions and premonitions to be correct, he needed them to be so.

'Talk about Lewis. Fight for him. Tell them what he drew on the beach that night. Make them understand it is all connected,' he said.

I climbed the steps and opened the small gate. The floor of the bandstand was littered with beer cans. Dr Black smiled and nodded to me, then started to clap. People looked towards us and for a second I was sure I glimpsed Lewis's pale face among them.

'Speak,' he said again.

'Lewis was a prophet,' I shouted.

And Dr Black clapped again, his face beaming, and turned his head to look behind him, gesturing to people with his arms. 'Trust yourself,' he said to me.

I shouted louder now. 'He knew what was coming and he predicted that something would happen to him. He told me he would die. Three weeks ago he sat in my garden and said those words.'

It felt like a betrayal of Lewis in some way.

'He knew the lights were watching him, watching all of us, from up there,' I shouted and pointed to the Ridge.

Dr Black folded his arms and watched the people as they gathered around us.

'If you are afraid of the lights, you are right to be so,' I went on.

A few people clapped and the crowd began to grow. They were listening, finally, and every one of them seemed to have Lewis's face.

Chapter Eighteen

My mother remained devastated about Lewis's disappearance and returned to her more normal, chaotic and silent self. Mr Bowen stayed working in his room most days, leaving only for a swim and their evenings in the garden. She was distracted, even with him, the kitchen messy, shopping forgotten, her canvas empty and soon to be stored away again. She cried on the phone to Lewis's mother and rang the guards every morning to check for news. Mr Bowen wondered if Lewis might have just left the town, he was an adult after all. She looked at him with disdain and then fled to the garden, a large straw hat and wine glass in hand. He stared at her through the window, before retreating up the stairs. I wondered if he might go off her, just pack up and leave early.

Marcus and I attempted to recover from the incident on the rocks. He called over with news of the kids in town, the latest theory about what had happened to Lewis which ranged from him being abducted by aliens, to being run over by the midnight freight train that passed through the town on its way to the city. His elation wasn't there though, the pent-up energy had subsided and he was more interested in talking about ways to find beer than the lights or any of my dreams any more.

There was a boredom to our conversations that hadn't been there before, and also a sense that he couldn't talk freely, a part of him held back. The boy who had crushed my hand in the dark and wept on the steps was truly gone. I wasn't as important to him as I had been, though he kept calling to the house. I tried to reconcile myself to this new order, but in between thoughts of Lewis it kept me awake at night and I contemplated ways to win him back. I thought I was the most interesting I had ever been that summer, alive and brave, and I wondered why he failed to notice.

We were looking through records in my room, sheltering from the heat of the afternoon. He was chewing gum and lying on my bed. The window was open behind him, the gauze curtain blowing out and catching on the window frame.

'You think he is dead?' His arm dangled down from the bed, his fingers tracing the gap between the floorboards.

I could make out the purple-and-black marks of the fake tattoo on his arm, still there, though faded now.

'I haven't dreamed of him but I feel it, there is an emptiness or something,' I replied, tears in my eyes.

'Those dolls are freaky.' He pointed to the shelf. 'They have dead eyes. Lewis had dead eyes too, did you ever notice that? Well, not dead, but you know what I mean.'

'That last night on the beach when I spoke to him, his eyes weren't dead, he was coming back to life,' I replied.

'What do you mean?'

'He seemed awake again, he understood what was going on,' I said, wiping my nose. Then I got up and looked for a tissue in my drawer. Marcus didn't seem to care that I was upset.

'The lights have stopped coming here, since he's been gone. It's almost a week now and no sighting,' he replied.

I looked up at the porcelain dolls on the shelf. They were covered in dust, all sagging satin hats and faded lace dresses, their ringlets matted and neglected. I didn't know why I kept them there, they should have been in the attic.

The phone rang downstairs, my mother was out in the garden and unaware.

'Some people, they think you're making it all up,' he said.

'You can't listen to other people, you have to trust yourself, trust me.'

'You have to listen to other people, or you end up like Lewis.'

'Lewis felt something up there too,' I said. 'He just couldn't find the right words – and why are you being so uncaring?'

Marcus's face paled and he looked briefly guilty and sorry for his words. His hand retreated from the floor and rested on the bed. 'I heard about the thing on the bandstand,' he said, sitting up.

'Yes?'

'I'm not sure you should talk like that.' He looked down at me.

He seemed worried, perplexed. It made me think he still might have cared, that his greater distance from me was borne of jealousy because I was sharing things with everyone and not just him any more. Perhaps it was I who had displaced us and not the other way round.

'I have to tell people. It's like a mission. Dr Black feels it too,' I said, getting up off the floor and sitting beside him on the edge of the bed.

He moved over and turned his face away to the window.

'Did you ever try and talk to Lewis about what happened to your dads?' I asked.

'No,' he said sharply, reaching out his arm to touch the curtain.

'I'm sorry, so sorry I didn't, I couldn't help that day they went out in the boat. I would have, I wanted to but it was too late,' I said.

'Don't talk about it, will you? You were never able to save them, stop thinking that you were.'

I held my breath but he didn't say anything else and a complicated silence filled the room. The phone had rung out downstairs, unanswered.

'I heard something about Mr Bowen,' he said, turning to me.

There were freckles on his cheeks and across his nose; his lips were dry and his mouth slightly open, he looked hot and thirsty. The night on the Ridge flicked into my mind, how close we had come to changing things. I reached up and touched the hard, shining stud in his ear. He didn't move but watched me closely, his eyes like bright, glittering jewels in his lovely face. He took my hand gently down from his ear and then looked at it a second, his golden head bowed, before gently laying it back on the bed.

'I have to go.' His face was red when he looked up.

'Don't, I want it. . . I did that night too on the Ridge,' I said, moving closer to him, our knees touching.

He got up suddenly and walked to the door. 'It's not right,' he said.

'Why?'

'I don't feel like that and everything's changed.'

I didn't believe him, he was just mistaken, confused, and in time he would see that. 'I haven't changed, not about you,' I said.

'You have,' he answered, leaving the room.

Chapter Nineteen

Mr Bowen had booked a restaurant outside town in an attempt to lighten the strange mood of the house. He told my mother about it late that afternoon, a look of expectation on his face.

'Natasha might like to come,' she said.

He blushed and looked vaguely dismayed though he tried to hide it.

We never went to restaurants. This one was expensive with large windows that faced out to the beach in a pretty village further up the coast. The tables were close together with red candles on each. A man played guitar in the corner and the room hummed with chattering people, tourists from the city, people with beach houses and a few locals. I recognized our solicitor and his very thin, expensively dressed wife.

Our table was very small because it was only meant for two so the staff began to hastily rearrange. My mother buried herself in a menu while Mr Bowen stared out to sea, avoiding my gaze. I wondered whether he was well off. I had never considered it before, he didn't seem so really, he didn't have a car for a start. He had travelled in Europe though; he told my mother about the places he had been when they were together in the evenings. His language about far-off cities was lyrical and I could feel the words sticking to her.

'I don't think we should be here,' my mother said finally, looking up.

Mr Bowen frowned and sat back in his chair, tilting it almost on its back legs.

'Because of Lewis?' I said, drinking water from a wine glass.

'Yes.' She nodded. Then shook her head as she said, 'I think of him day and night – the thought of him lost somewhere and scared, or worse. . .'

She was looking pale, circles under her eyes. Mr Bowen fiddled with his knife and tried to get the waiter's attention.

'We can go,' he said finally.

'I'm sort of hungry,' I replied.

He looked from one of us to the other and took his hand off the knife.

'Well, let's stay then.' He turned again to see if we could order food.

The local solicitor approached the table. He was quite young and had inherited the practice from his father. He was getting fat, also like his father, and there was sweat on his forehead. My mother had told me he had once asked her to a dance and written her love letters. He shook hands with Mr Bowen, a look of smug scepticism on his face.

'Elizabeth, we never see you,' he said, ignoring me and fixing on her.

She blushed and looked down at her hands.

'You know what I'm like,' she said, finally raising her green eyes.

'I do,' he said, looking frostily at Mr Bowen.

She was public property in a way in the town. The therapist looks sceptical when I say this but I believe it to be true. It was a different time, and she had failed a test of respectability, and her very presence stimulated thought and comment as a result, but because she was so beautiful and the family had once been important they could not discard her completely. Instead they watched her closely and their gaze became a kind of prison, her beauty and her perceived moral failures a magnet to all kinds of judgement.

'You know, there isn't a week that goes by when someone doesn't ask me if they can buy that beautiful house of yours. The town is changing, lots of new people and money coming in,' the solicitor said.

'It's very expensive to keep and there's damp on the walls,' I replied.

He looked at me and his eyes were drained of interest.

'Hear you're a bit of a celebrity these days, Natasha,' he said, an eyebrow raised.

He pointed to the far corner of the restaurant where, sitting at the table next to his wife, was Amy Martin, the TV reporter who had called to our house. They were in animated conversation.

'We would never sell the house,' said my mother.

Mr Bowen watched her intently as she spoke. He hated this man at our table, I could sense a burning anger in him. He would not look at the solicitor and if he moved a foot closer to her he would have kicked him away.

'I thought as much. That's what I tell them when they ask – some things never change. Lovely to see you though, don't be a stranger.' He walked away then.

'How alarming,' she said.

'It's his job really, don't think anything of it.' Mr Bowen reached out to touch her hand. 'You belong in that house,' he added.

The waiter arrived and we ordered some drinks. Mr Bowen looked more relaxed and drank his beer, his quizzical gaze occasionally resting on other people in the restaurant. My mother was telling him about something that had happened at the shops earlier in the day, making fun of herself. Mr Bowen stopped her when she did this, a deft deflection. He wanted to prevent her from slipping into the abyss. I recognized the action because I used to do the same, a valiant but ultimately hopeless effort to save her from going under.

'I have to go back to the city for a few days,' Mr Bowen said hesitantly.

'When?' I asked.

He ignored me and the hum of the room grew. No one came to take our order. Men looked sunburned, women whispered in their ears and discreetly took ownership of the wine bottles perched on the tables. My mother and Mr Bowen didn't seem to notice the delay. The reporter from the TV station began weaving her way towards us.

'Hello again.' Amy smiled at Mr Bowen, then turned in my direction. 'I couldn't get a room in town, in the end. We came for the story about the lights, but we stayed on a few days to see if anything happens with the missing boy. We thought there might be a link or some angle.' She was talking only to me now.

'There really isn't, I'm sure,' my mother said, her glass in hand.

'Such a lot of stuff going on in a small town, though. There is a lot of interest in the place. We just did an interview with Dr Black, you know him, I think?'

I nodded.

'He's really great, such an interesting guy, and he has a lot of time for you.'

Mr Bowen rose suddenly from his seat then, his chair hitting off the table behind. He turned briefly to apologize to the other diner. 'We were actually about to leave, we thought we had time for dinner, but we didn't in the end,' he said awkwardly.

'Oh OK, well, I would love to talk again, I might call at the house,' Amy said.

My mother rose too. She looked exotic and beautifully aggressive. I could see people in the room turn to watch her. It was always the way.

'There really would be no point, we have no vacancies at the moment,' she said, leaving her napkin down.

Mr Bowen let her pass, hurriedly paid the waiter and followed her out the door. I could see his back straighten, his shoulders broaden the closer he got to her, he was basking in the attention directed at her, like she was a prize that he had won.

'I'll talk to you,' I said, squeezing out from behind the table and watching them retreat through the door.

Amy smiled triumphantly at me, all perfect teeth and coral lipstick.

'Tomorrow,' she said, nodding.

When I got outside, my mother and Mr Bowen had wandered off the terrace and onto the beach, a strong but warm breeze had picked up and the sand seemed to rise and fall around them. They walked away slowly, deep in conversation; the sky above their heads was mauve, with dark clouds on the far horizon.

I wondered what it was that Marcus had wanted to tell me about him.

Chapter Twenty

The next morning Lewis's bike was found in a lonely field the other side of the Ridge; it was the lead item on the local news. He had been missing for almost ten days now. Amy was on the screen, shots of thick, lush hedgerows and a cornfield in the background. She finished by saying that people were becoming increasingly nervous, and the camera moved to rest on a group of onlookers who were pointing over a fence.

Mr Bowen was leaving for the city that morning, a small overnight bag packed and left beside the front door. I could hear him talking to my mother upstairs as I went out into the garden. It was warm, but the sky was a pale grey. The cat sat beside the hedge, its paw raised, ready to catch an unsuspecting mouse.

'If you know anything, have heard anything from those kids on the beach, you need to say,' said Mr Bowen from behind me.

He was dressed formally in a suit, bag in hand.

'They don't tell me anything,' I replied.

'It's serious about Lewis,' he said.

I noticed my mother at the window upstairs staring at us. She lifted her hand to wave in a sort of lost, sad fashion.

'I read Black's book, there's some strange stuff in there,' he said.

He noticed me looking at the window behind him, turned and waved back at her.

'It's only strange if you have a closed mind,' I said.

'There are question marks hanging over a lot of his academic work.' He walked to the gate. 'You know there is no hidden hand deciding things.'

'I don't need you to believe,' I replied.

'Best to be honest with each other, I think.'

The pale blue sky was empty and vast behind him.

'I am being honest. I warned Lewis he was in danger, and I warned you,' I said.

He shook his head and disappeared down the steps.

Perhaps there was no hidden hand, just imperfect choices.

∗ ∗ ∗

There were extra guards monitoring the town, interviewing people and handing out leaflets. The path to the Ridge was clogged with cars parked up and small groups of volunteers talking, heads bowed before walking into the woods at the start of the trail. The tourists seemed muted somehow, watching from the cafés, their colourful T-shirts and shorts inappropriately joyous. They had been catapulted into a mystery and were not prepared.

Amy was waiting for me in the hotel, seated near the window. I noticed Dr Black talking to the receptionist in the corner. 'I think the lights that came, I think they were calling him,' I said.

She put her cup of coffee down on the glass table. 'Calling Lewis?' she said, eyebrows raised.

'He was confused, but something was calling him up there and he was both afraid and drawn to it.'

'You saw the lights yourself too?'

'Yes,' I replied.

'What do you think they are?' she asked.

'I don't know, something not of this world.'

'Really?' She leaned forward.

Dr Black had finished with the receptionist and was staring at me, a look of concern on his elegant face. He seemed diminished, smaller somehow at this distance, his hat under his arm.

'Did you know there were sightings like this here before?' she said, nibbling the top of her pen.

'I had heard that.'

'Yes, it has happened twice before – 1949 and 1962. I spoke to Jim in the caravan park about it and then checked it out with local newspapers from the time.'

'I don't know much about it,' I answered.

'A woman and her daughter claimed to have seen them hover over their farm one night before disappearing at speed, and in the other case which I thought was interesting, it was a group of scouts that were camping on the Ridge. They weren't from the area so didn't know of the earlier experience.'

'Did people believe them?' I asked.

'Well, the woman sold up and left a year or so after. She was a widow and claimed to have been too afraid to stay there any longer. She thought they might come back. There were suggestions she was chased out too, by her neighbours – was made to feel uncomfortable.'

'Does Mike Ryan know about this? He would like to know, I'd say.'

She smiled and laid down her notebook. 'I'm sure he does, he's busy with what's happening now though so maybe isn't visiting the library.' She winked at me.

'He doesn't seem a library type of man.'

'Can I ask, was Lewis ever with you on the Ridge?'

I shook my head. 'He tried to tell me what he saw but we weren't there together. He drew it for me too,' I said.

'Do you think he went searching for them the night he went missing?'

'Yes. I left him on the beach and he ran in that direction.'

'You saw him that night?' she asked.

I nodded.

'I heard he had been beaten up, did you know that?'

'Yes,' I replied.

'Do you know who it was that did it?'

I shook my head, then jumped. Dr Black had put his hand on the back of my chair. The reporter looked up and offered him her brightest smile.

'May I?' he said, gesturing to the seat.

'But you do know some of the boys who are being questioned?' she asked.

'I didn't know anyone was being questioned,' I replied.

'A few days before Lewis's disappearance a child claimed to have been followed and chased on the Ridge. They want to talk to some of the same youths about that too,' she finished.

'I expect they do,' said Dr Black.

'It's an odd place, the Ridge,' I said.

They both looked at me.

'What do you mean?' she asked.

'It's always been that way, and the lights appearing there just confirms it. It's a haunted place,' I said.

Some children were spinning the revolving door of the hotel and laughing. The reporter looked unsure, confused slightly. She sat back then and took a drink of her coffee, glancing briefly to Dr Black.

'The circumstances of the boy's departure are indeed concerning. Natasha is, I imagine, trying to give you some insight into Lewis's state of mind before he went missing,' he said.

He was wearing a large platinum ring with an aquamarine stone on one of his fingers. It reminded me of the colour of Marcus's eyes.

The journalist looked at his hand and shifted uncomfortably in her seat. 'I'm not sure we can go any further right now, but thank you, Natasha, for talking to me.' She gathered her things off the table between us.

'This girl has powers of precognition, she is an empath also,' Dr Black said.

The woman stopped still and stared at him, her eyes narrowing slightly.

'She absorbs people's energies,' he explained. 'The world is a highly charged experience for people like Natasha. She can sense the feelings and emotions of others, is attuned to their soul wounds and sometimes, sometimes, she can see things before they happen, she has a sense of what is going to befall them.'

An empath, a word that didn't denote fairground attractions and women in headscarves, a crystal ball in their hands.

'To some degree we are all of us connected, and a person like Natasha can actually sense it, feel it as real as anything. This is not an abstract philosophy for her, or some pointless distraction. She is trying to help you in her own way, and deserves only your respect, though whether you choose to believe is of course entirely up to you,' he said.

'That's interesting and I'm grateful for your time and insight, Natasha,' she said uncomfortably.

'Is someone sick?' I said suddenly.

Amy's eyes became wide and fearful. I could hear crying around her, in her, someone struggling to hold her hand and then fading, slipping away.

'In your family maybe?' I said. 'Something with skin.' I showed her my hands that I had rubbed raw as we spoke.

'Yes,' she said, sinking down onto the seat.

I took her hand which was cool, perfumed and soft.

'My mother has cancer,' she said quietly.

Dr Black was smiling sadly and tapping the ring on his finger, over and over.

'I don't talk about it much, we are very close and I can't imagine losing her,' she said, gulping.

Her mother would die, she did not have long left but there was nothing to be gained by sharing this.

'I'm so sorry. My mother is my world,' I whispered.

She took out a tissue and wiped her eyes, then sipped her drink. She watched me over the glass before leaving a few minutes later, looking back over her shoulder as she disappeared through the revolving doors.

'When you let people in, Natasha, the more they see you, the more they believe,' Dr Black said.

I sat back against the leather chair, exhausted suddenly. I had never done that before, told a complete stranger so clearly and exactly what I knew about them. It felt both liberating and draining.

'But does it actually help anyone to know?' I asked.

'Let's have some wine.' He clicked his fingers at one of the waiters and ordered a bottle.

'I'm too young.'

'Nonsense, this is a special occasion, a coming-of-age party of sorts. Let's be Mediterranean.'

'I don't think so.'

'So moral,' he replied. 'I respect that about you, a puritan of the soul.'

'No, an angel of doom.' I reluctantly took the glass offered.

'Someone has to be,' he replied.

The wine was sweet.

Chapter Twenty-One

When I left the hotel, Marcus was outside laughing, a skateboard at his feet. A few girls sat on the wall behind him eating ice pops, legs swinging. He looked taller, his shoulders broad in his tight T-shirt, and his hair was shaved closer and bleached peroxide white. He was embarrassed when I walked over to him, the laughter stopped and he cast a quick glance at the other girls.

'I dyed it,' he said before I could ask.

'You are pretty,' I said, laughing.

The girls whispered to each other.

'Have you been drinking?' He looked around furtively.

'A small bit.'

He led me away from the promenade and onto the beach towards the rocks at the foot of the Ridge. The girls watched us go, and some of them laughed out loud then. My head was dizzy as we walked, I stumbled and he grabbed my arm.

'Victoria said I should do it,' he said.

'Do what?'

'My hair.'

'You'll definitely get an invitation to her party this year,' I replied, shoving him.

'I might be like you, and not go,' he said, kicking sand.

The sun was breaking through the clouds, children were scampering between buckets of water, sandcastles and giant holes they had dug in the sand.

'No, you'll go,' I said.

I wanted to ask him why he liked the girls on the wall, as if I was a scientist examining the channels of his heart – I already knew what was in his soul – but even slightly drunk, something held me back.

'Still no lights.' He looked sideways at me.

'No,' I replied.

'For good?'

'I don't know.'

'There are always predictions about the end of the world, and it never seems to happen,' he said.

'Perhaps I am a complete charlatan and have failed all your tests,' I added.

He didn't answer, just kicked some more sand.

'Why are you doubting me all the time now?' I pushed him in the shoulder again.

'I'm not. You're just a bit drunk.'

The rowers carried a boat out ahead of us on their shoulders.

The sea was starting to glint, the sun beginning to burn through the clouds.

'No, not drunk, just happy, happy because I am free.' I twirled in the sand.

He smiled and for a minute it seemed like we were back, like it was before. I wanted to put my arms around his neck, touch his shaved head and pull him down into the sand. Taste him. I had tasted wine, but never him, and it seemed wrong.

'That thing about Mr Bowen,' he said. He looked uneasy and anxious, frowning and rubbing his white hair.

I stopped spinning but my head kept turning. I leaned down. He rested his hand on my back as I looked at my toes encased in the damp sand.

'Victoria says her father knows him in the city, and he's married. Everyone is talking about it,' he said.

I didn't feel surprised, not then. It was almost a relief. I didn't need to be guilty about disliking him and wanting him gone. I wondered briefly if that was the meaning of my dream, that it wasn't about his death but rather his deception.

'So he is a liar and a cheat,' I said, standing up straight and covering my eyes from the sun.

I could see Mr Bowen lying in the grass with my mother, looking up at the sky, the pages of his book scattered all around them. All the sweet words on his tongue and lies in his heart.

'Yeah,' said Marcus. 'I thought you should know, hear about it from me,' he added.

'Thanks,' I said, my voice faint.

'Will you tell her?' he said.

I started to feel sick and covered my mouth with my hand.

'He's making a fool of her, Victoria said that,' he said. 'Are you OK?'

I bit my lip and nodded. I couldn't get sick in front of him.

'I've got to go back now.' He gestured to the promenade. He was always leaving, walking away.

'I thought we might. . .' I reached out to touch his arm. I could hear the expectancy in my voice and pitied myself and felt again like I would vomit.

'I said I'd go back to them,' he answered. He gestured again to the seafront and the girls who were still sitting on the wall. The girls who waited for him, the girls who would always wait for him. I could see a long line of them stretching out into his future. He would have a life filled with touch, whispers and admiration.

I tried to think of something to say that would keep him with me, but nothing came. There were no dreams, no visions that could hold him, and if I tried to speak only my insides would come out and he didn't want to see that.

'Go, I'm OK,' I said.

I watched him walk away, his head down, and a part of me believed I would never see him again. He didn't care about Lewis and he didn't want to be seen with me any more. Even my superpower gift could not keep him and everything was changed.

I sank into the wet sand, laid my hot cheek into its coolness and thought perhaps the end of the world took many forms.

* * *

My mother was sketching, sitting cross-legged on the rug when I finally got home. The wine of earlier had left only a headache and a sense of foolishness. There were occasional shouts and roars from the seafront far below, the amusements were alive and pounding the air with whistles and sirens. The air smelled sweet, the honeysuckle behind her was so overgrown it looked like it might collapse, the trellis too weak to hold its abundance.

'The sun came back. A grey day feels like an affront now. I can't imagine how we will cope with winter this year,' she said.

Two long black plaits hung down under her straw hat, a book of poetry by Thomas Hardy lay on the rug, charcoal pencils strewn everywhere. She looked like a child and I felt a sense of pity for her and all that she did not know.

'What are you drawing?' I sat down beside her.

'Oh, nothing really, I can't concentrate any more, there's still no news of him and it's just unbelievable.'

I leaned down to look more closely at the pad, and saw the outline of a thin man sitting on a beach.

'I didn't feel like painting, drawing is more therapeutic, simpler,' she explained.

'Do you miss him?' I asked.

She pulled her hat down slightly, the pattern of the straw like a lattice on her face, her eyes unavailable, in retreat.

'Lewis? Of course.'

'No, Mr Bowen.'

'He will be back in a day or so,' she answered swiftly.

She continued drawing and the cat wandered out from the house, into the long yellow grass and towards the orchard.

'They found Lewis's bike.' I picked at the daisies.

'I know, I spoke to his mother this morning. She is almost broken with grief and I don't know what to say to her.' She looked up briefly.

'What's Mr Bowen doing in the city?'

'Working,' she replied, looking down to her sketchpad again.

'Don't you think we should vet people before they come to stay?' I asked.

'We run a bed and breakfast, not a secret society.'

'You didn't want the TV lady to stay. So you do apply some standards as to who you allow here.'

'Natasha, don't start again about him. He will be gone in a few weeks, it's almost August.'

'When are you going to admit that you have feelings for him?' I asked.

She put the sketchpad and pencil down. 'There is nothing between Mr Bowen and me. We are friends.' She pulled her knees up and hugged them.

'Isn't there? Marcus said you were seen kissing him, and I saw you holding hands on the beach outside that restaurant.' The words came rushing out. 'The whole town knows and you say nothing to me.'

'That's just gossip,' she said, eyebrows raised.

'You are either lying to me or to yourself.'

'Don't speak to me like that,' she replied, getting to her feet.

I picked up her sketchpad. 'Tell me then, who is this?' I held it up to her.

'It's Lewis,' she said quietly. She folded her arms and looked out to sea.

'I've seen you together here. I'm not a fool.'

'And what if I do have feelings for him?' she answered. 'Could you try and understand, the way I try and understand your stuff? It isn't exactly easy for me with you.'

'Do you think I'm crazy?' I asked, standing too.

'No.' She stretched out her hand. 'Could you be happy for me?' Her voice was soft, nervous.

'I don't think he's worthy of you. And could you try and think about me, what I'm going through at the moment?' I shouted.

I could feel tears in my eyes and for some reason it was Marcus and Lewis I saw, not Mr Bowen, and both of them were walking away, leaving me behind.

'I think of almost nothing else, you and Lewis,' she said.

'The kids no one wanted, whose fathers left them.'

She looked startled. 'Stop,'

I thought if I could drive her to tears, she could cry them for me.

She gripped my arm tight and then pulled me close.

'Nothing will ever change the way we love each other,' she said.

'Do you mean it?'

'If the heavens fell in on us, nothing would change how I feel, ever.'

She paused for a second, I could hear the bees hovering over the lavender pots.

'And no one will ever separate us?' I asked. Tell me I'm the centre of your universe.

'Never, not even the end of the world.'

I didn't believe her though, I never did. I remained the child who followed her around the house just in case this was the day she would leave.

'Can you ask him not to come back, for me?' I asked.

'No, I can't do that,' she replied quietly.

I wanted to tell her Mr Bowen was a liar, belonged to someone else, but could not do it yet, and instead collapsed against her, and started to cry.

'I'm lonely sometimes, we both are,' she whispered into my hair.

'Marcus doesn't like me any more,' I said.

She loosened her hug and took my face in her hands. 'I'm sure that's not true.'

'He prefers the others, and he doesn't care about Lewis.'

'Maybe he's growing up a bit, wants to do his own thing more. He does care about Lewis, we all do, and no one knows what to say about it. We are all scared.' She wiped a tear from my eye.

'If I looked like you, it wouldn't have happened, Marcus would not have left. He would love me,' I said.

'You are lovely. And Marcus hasn't left, Lewis has.'

'That's not true,' I answered. 'A beautiful face is a magical thing, more magical than seeing the future.'

'Maybe it's time to find some new friends, try and forget everything – the future, the dreams, pretend they don't matter for a time. Think about them when you are ready, when you know who you are. Don't let them define you.' There was a desperate plea in her voice.

'I don't have friends. I have followers and it's better than nothing,' I replied, pushing her away and walking into the house.

Perhaps it was the fate of all mothers and daughters, one must kill the spirit of the other. It was a necessary act of survival, and only one of us could triumph. I saw my need as far greater than hers and justified it because Mr Bowen was a cheat, and a liar. How happy could they have been? All of his admiration was built on a lie and he would make a fool of her.

And I needed her to mind me and dutiful though she tried to be, I never really felt looked after. Something about her was always elsewhere.

I went upstairs and roughly opened the door to Mr Bowen's room. He had left it tidy, the bed made and his clothes cleared away; his writing was stacked in piles on his desk, reference books on the floor, and a folded bit of paper propped up the dodgy leg of the desk. He had hung her painting of the beach over his bed, while a small black-and-white photo stood on his bedside table. It was of a woman in a flowery dress, holding the reins of a donkey; a small boy, Mr Bowen I presumed, was perched on top. Another summer, from a long time ago. I opened the drawers beside his bed, but they were empty, the large suitcase was locked and the papers on his desk were all covered in handwritten notes about dead soldiers. He had left no evidence of his other life.

I lay down on his bed.

Chapter Twenty-Two

I must have slept for when I woke the light in his room was dim, the air damp. The clock downstairs chimed eight o'clock, but it felt much later. I looked out the window to find that the house was wrapped in a thick sea mist, only the tip of the Ridge visible in the distance, a deep purple against the vaporous grey of the sky. I could vaguely hear the shipping news on the radio in the kitchen, strange words about moderate winds and extended outlooks, drifting upwards in the quiet still of the house.

I had a sudden sense that I was not alone. The room was filled with the smell of coconut and wet earth, just like on the Ridge. Lewis was near, I knew it, standing outside in the hall, his face pale, with eyes burning. I could hear heavy, laboured breaths through the wall and imagined his white hands, unsure on the door handle. He had travelled long and far to find me and his exhaustion was seeping in under the door. I tiptoed quietly over and pressed my head against it, willing him to speak.

'Lewis. Tell me where you are,' I whispered.

His breaths were shallow, fast now as if he had been running, escaping someone or something.

'Lewis, I saw your father the day he drowned, I saw his boat and I wanted to save him but I couldn't and no one would have believed me, and I am so very sorry for you and Marcus, and I wish I could change it, but I can help you now, this time. Just tell me, tell me, did the boys on the beach hurt you, did they chase you on the Ridge, were you following the lights, did they make you scared?' I said desperately.

But he didn't answer. Ghosts never talked to me.

I heard light footsteps walking slowly away then and the creak of the stairs. I opened the door gently. The landing was empty and dark, all the bedroom doors shut, and the radio downstairs was louder now, playing jazz. I trailed my hand along the uneven surface of the wall as I walked down the stairs and thought of the solicitor and all the rich people he knew who wanted to buy us out, to stop the house from decaying and to live fabulous lives in the house. And how Lewis would haunt them, he would stay in the house looking for my mother, roaming the hall and the garden.

She was curled up on one of the dainty French chairs in the front room, a low lamp on the table beside her. The wallpaper behind her head was cherry coloured, with the repeated pattern of a lady dancing under a ruined folly. The garden was a tropical jungle outside the window, all tangled, profuse dark greenery pressing against the glass, hanging heavy and swollen in the damp evening air.

Her face was mottled, as if she had been crying. A bottle of wine was open on the coffee table, an empty glass stood next to a book about Matisse and three tall red candles were lit. They flickered and danced, leaving patterns on the wall.

She leaned over to the table and poured herself more wine. The smell made me feel nauseous. I looked at myself in the mirror over the fireplace.

'Mr Bowen won't be back for a few days,' she said. 'You will be relieved.' She took a sip of the wine, then looked at me, her eyes serious. 'Are you still upset about Marcus?'

'What's it like to be beautiful?' I said, staring at my reflection. I thought about my father when I looked at myself. My hair was lighter than my mother's, my skin not quite so dark, my eyes a pale blue, not green. I was like a dissolved version of her, one that had been weakened by the blood and colour of someone else, a man who was missing. His act of creation forgotten.

She took another drink from her glass and wiped her mouth with her hand. 'I wouldn't know.' She lay her head back on the headrest of the chair.

The chipped gold leaf at her neck made her look even more regal than usual.

'When people look at me, it's different to the way they look at you,' I replied.

She rested her eyes on the unlit chandelier that was covered in stray dust and cobwebs, another of our housekeeping jobs left undone. The house was slipping downwards again, no one here to try and impress with Mr Bowen away.

'It's like pity and disappointment, sometimes scorn, though they try to cover it up. It's the same look they have when they find out I have no father,' I said.

'I can't control how other people look at you. Perhaps telling them about the end of the world, and ghosts floating in trees, contributes to the way they see you.' She took another drink.

There was the faint sound of rain against the window.

'It's not my job to make people feel better about themselves. That role is already taken – by you.' I turned from the mirror to look at her.

'You won't give up about Seán, will you?' she said.

Her face was flushed and her desperate need for me to approve of Mr Bowen had slipped into resentment.

'Did he explain why he is delayed?' I asked.

'Do you trust anyone? You will breed sad sorrows for yourself living without trust.'

I wanted to tell her what I had found out about Mr Bowen, but something held me back. I wanted him there to hear the words. It was he who should be humiliated, not her.

'And who taught me not to trust?' I asked instead. 'If I am only barely half alive it is because you taught me to be so.

All the people we don't talk to, rush past, keep our distance from. . . what are you afraid of?'

She sat up then, and rubbed her eyes. 'I apologize for all my flaws and failings that have had such an impact on you.'

There was a loud banging at the door and she checked the time but neither of us moved to answer.

'I thought I felt Lewis earlier.' I looked back at myself in the mirror. 'He was upstairs, looking for us, looking for you.'

Her green eyes looked large and fearful suddenly, like a sleek black cat that had been startled on its quiet stroll through a secluded garden. The knocking started again, a deep thudding.

'It means he's dead,' I said.

I could feel tears rise behind my eyes and an emptiness inside. I had known it for the last ten days, he was gone. He would never again sit with us in the garden.

'They never speak to me, the dead, and I don't know why. I saw Marcus's father too, the other week, but he didn't speak either. They just come and then go. I don't know what it is they want.'

'You are scaring me – stop.' She got up swiftly then and left for the hall to answer the door.

I could hear Dr Black's voice and smelled earth and rain.

'What a night, the weather's breaking,' he said, leaning his umbrella against the sitting-room door.

She gave me a fearful glance and offered him a glass of wine.

He settled into the couch. 'I apologize for the late call.'

'He's dead,' I said.

Dr Black laid his glass down and my mother walked to the window.

'Lewis,' I said.

'You saw, felt something?' he asked, sitting forward.

'Yes.'

There was a sudden draught of cold air in the room, the door creaked open and we heard the sound of something heavy banging at the back of the house.

'Those damn French doors,' my mother said, her voice breaking as if she were about to cry. She left swiftly to close them.

Dr Black watched her leave, before getting up and walking over to me at the fireplace.

'Can you tell where he is?' he asked.

His eyes were black in the low light and he stood close to me, watching my lips as if I might start speaking in tongues. Perhaps he would have liked that.

'Is there anything you could offer the guards that would help, not just Lewis, but you, both of us?' he said.

'Help?' I answered.

'Yes, anything that might identify where he is?' he explained.

'It's not like that.' I shook my head.

The rain was heavier outside now.

'Like in Italy,' he said, glancing back to the window. 'Those hot, hot weeks that break with fire and rain. I spent a summer in Venice. The most haunted of cities.' He turned to look at me.

There was the low sound of thunder far off down the coast.

'I can try and talk to him, if he comes again, but I don't really know how, it's not something I've done. It's different to the dreams,' I said.

'Perhaps we can look to arrange something, a way of reaching out to him,' he said. 'If we could find something to help the guards in their search, it would raise your standing, really show them who you are, the powers you have. As well as helping the poor boy's family, obviously.'

My mother pushed open the door. She looked afraid, her face pale. 'There was someone in the garden,' she said faintly.

Dr Black rose quickly and gestured to me to direct him. We walked through the hall and I looked briefly up the stairs. The landing was dark above us; we continued on to the back of the house and into the dining room. I went to turn the light on, but he shook his head. The French doors were secured, the drapes pulled back; the trees of the orchard twisted in the grey, wet evening, fruit and leaves strewn in the thick grass. The mist was thicker now, the gate to the cliff steps had vanished in the grey of the evening. Dr Black put his hand on the door handle but did not attempt to open them.

'It was in the orchard, I saw a shadow move through the trees,' she said behind us.

The rain was still beating heavily against the glass. Water gushed out of the broken gutters overhead, pouring down the side of the house and pooling between the uneven paving stones, and the sky above was heavy and low with black clouds. The garden looked deserted and lonely and like my mother, unprepared, dismayed at summer's end. We stayed there in silence a moment.

'The guards interviewed your friend about Lewis. The fair-haired boy,' Dr Black said, turning to me.

AUGUST

Chapter Twenty-Three

I slept late the next morning. The sun was already high but pale coming through the curtains, the wind and rain of last night had gone, like a storm imagined. Dust floated in the sunbeams that struck the wall, the dead-eyed dolls on the shelf above looked down at me, their faces solemn. I could hear Dr Black's deep voice in the kitchen below. He had stayed over, the weather too wild to walk back to the hotel. They were drinking coffee. The room was filled with a thin sunshine, the window open, the breeze cool and the low hum of the seafront faintly audible.

'We will arrange it for tonight – the seance,' he said, looking at me.

My mother rose from the table and got juice out of the fridge. She looked as if she had not slept much, grey circles under her eyes and her hair dragged up in a high severe bun.

'Your mother is very supportive. If we can help shed some light on Lewis's whereabouts. . . we have a responsibility to help.' He glanced at her, an earnest expression on his face.

She nodded while pouring out a glass. I had the sense that she had given up under the lyrical pressure of Dr Black and his endless belief in me.

'It has to be here,' she said.

He nodded. 'Of course, his presence was here,' he assured her.

I noticed she shuddered briefly and turned as if someone was behind her.

'I don't know what to do, I've never tried to contact them. . . not on purpose,' I said. And for the first time I was afraid and saw my gift as an endless burden.

'I will lead, you follow,' he said.

The phone rang then and my mother disappeared into the hall.

I sat down. 'Do you know what happened at the interviews with the guards?'

'Only barely. Mike Ryan knows more and I will meet him this morning. It seems a group of youths were interviewed again, they were seen on the Ridge the night Lewis disappeared and there is a belief they know more about what happened than they are admitting,' he explained.

'Marcus told me he saw Lewis that night, but he said it was on the beach.'

'It may well have been, who knows at this point?' he said, getting up from the chair.

'Marcus wouldn't hurt him, he is gentle with others. Not himself, he's always hurting himself, but with other people. . .'

I gazed out the window. 'I can't believe Lewis is really gone, I want to be wrong.'

He sighed and laid his cup down on the table. 'Thank your mother for me, and I will be back at eight tonight.'

Lewis was someone we loved. I wanted to say this, explain it to him but didn't.

'You should never want to be wrong, not when your abilities are so special,' he said, pausing at the door.

'Is there something I should do to prepare?' I asked.

'No, leave it all to me, just stay open, as you were last evening. It is what is so enchanting about you.' He smiled at me.

My mother finished her call and sat back down at the table. Dr Black bade us farewell and let himself out the front door.

'Was it Lewis you thought you saw in the garden?' I asked.

'I don't know, for an instant I thought it was Seán,' she said, frowning. 'It was such a strange evening, I'm sorry we fought.'

'Was that him on the phone?'

'Yes, he's still in the city and most definitely not prowling our garden.' She touched the rim of her cup with her fingers.

'Do you love him?' I asked. The words forced themselves out – she owed me the truth, or so I felt. I could not surmise and suspect any more.

'I don't know,' she said faintly.

I cleared Dr Black's place quickly from the table, dumping crockery loudly in the sink. It was so completely the kind of answer she would give, but then I thought about Marcus and how I had not known I loved him until it was too late. There was perhaps something wrong and slow with both of us.

'I'm sorry,' she said.

I hate to think of her apologizing now. I have spent a lot of my life assuming I was the one who was wronged but when I revisit that time, go back over it all, I become afraid that I was the monster. All my fears and insecurities were escaping in the heat of that summer and overpowering everyone. I was unforgiving, driven by a zeal for something I still do not fully understand. My therapist takes notes and nods at me, willing me on to the great awakening she believes I am still capable of.

'Why don't you seem happier, then?' I asked my mother.

'Happy! Who can be happy now with Lewis. . . And meeting Seán changes things, and I know how you don't want him here. And it scares me,' she replied.

'Why?' I asked.

I turned to face her, she was leaning her head against her hand, propped up on the table.

'Because I've tried not to need people since. . .' She faltered over the words.

My father and his paint-covered knife.

'It doesn't have to change things, you can refuse, and he might not love you, he might not want you,' I said. 'He could be pretending.'

She looked at me sadly. 'He doesn't do that, he's not like that,' she replied.

I still couldn't tell her. He needed to be there when I said the words, it was to be his punishment for falling in love with a woman he should not have.

I never thought about what revealing his secret would do to her, not then anyway.

* * *

Victoria's holiday house was slightly smaller than our home, a double-fronted Edwardian villa, one-storey over a basement, painted a very pale pink with wrought-iron window boxes and a purple clematis draped over the front porch. At the side of the house, almost out of sight, there were canoes stacked up with wetsuits drying on top. A French au pair opened the front door, a thin cigarette in her hand. She pointed down the hall. Victoria was curled up on a couch in the small conservatory at the back of the house, almost hidden among potted plants, a Walkman on and reading *The Outsiders*.

'I've seen the film,' I said.

'The book is so much better.' She took off her headphones. 'She was only seventeen when it was published, imagine,' she said, putting them down on the wicker table between us. 'I would adore to write a book one day.' She stayed lying on the couch as she spoke.

'Marcus told me about Mr Bowen and I wanted to find out more,' I said.

She sat up then and folded her legs under her. 'I didn't know whether to tell you or not.' She frowned and looked around the room. 'I wish I could smoke.'

She seemed so mature and worldly for her age, I wondered what Marcus thought when she spoke so, what went through his head as he looked at her.

'Who is he married to?' I asked.

'Oh, I have no idea, it's my father who knows him vaguely from somewhere,' she replied, turning back to me. 'Marcus was really annoyed about it, he wants to beat him up,' she said, her blue eyes wide.

I smiled faintly.

'Will you tell her?' she asked.

'I have to.'

'Perhaps you could confront him first, see what he says?' she said, leaning forward. 'Maybe he truly loves her. You can marry the wrong person I think and be searching and then he meets your mother and this was meant to be. . .'

'He's a liar,' I said.

And he was, and I didn't really think love could matter more than truth, though it was to be the lesson of that summer in a way.

'My mother would call him a cad – such an odd word really when you think about it. She doesn't really believe in romance and people being star-crossed,' she said.

'I agree with your mother,' I replied.

'I don't – I believe everyone has a soulmate.'

'I'd better go,' I replied, standing up.

'We're going diving later, Marcus and a few of the others,' she said casually.

'I can't swim.'

'I know, Marcus said that.' She picked up the headphones and lay down on the couch again, her head turned towards me. 'Have you seen his hair? It looks really cool.'

'Yes.'

I looked around the room, it had a huge bay window that faced out to the train station and the sea beyond. The wallpaper was gold and there were large paintings of ships in full sail on stormy oceans, the couches were red and plumped fat with giant cushions. It was the opposite of our threadbare sitting room.

'He's very good-looking, don't you think?' She had an impish look on her face.

'I've never thought about it.' I walked to the door.

'Why haven't you?' she asked.

'We're just friends, not even that now really.' I looked out to the patio.

The au pair was still smoking while picking up some wet towels and goggles discarded on the grass.

'What do you mean?' she asked. She looked surprised, a spark of deep interest and intrigue in her blue eyes.

'He's scared,' I answered.

'He's in love more likely.'

And for a second I thought she meant with me, and I felt a kind of joy rising before I remembered the other girl.

'I have the best bit of gossip,' she said, sitting up again and crossing her legs. 'Marcus and the girl, the one you saw going into the cave. . .'

Despite myself I nodded for her to continue.

'Well, the other night, they were together on the Ridge for ages and. . . they are going out with each other now,' she said, blushing.

'You don't know that they are,' I said.

There was an actual pain in my chest, it must have been my heart. It felt like it was collapsing downwards to the floor.

'Everyone is talking about what they did up there,' she said, giggling. 'I'm not sure it's that big an achievement but there you go.' She lay down again.

'I need to leave,' I said.

'Sure.'

I hated him most completely in that moment.

'Did you know Marcus was interviewed about Lewis?' I asked.

'They were all interviewed.' She sounded bored now.

'Do they know anything about what happened to him?'

She had started putting her headphones back on and was fiddling with the buttons on the machine. 'I don't know, weird stuff happens up there on the Ridge,' she said.

'Don't you care at all?' I asked.

'I didn't know the boy, he was just someone from the beach really.' Turning up the volume, she closed her eyes.

Chapter Twenty-Four

Dr Black was sitting at the dining-room table, my mother leaning against the sideboard behind him, a cup of coffee in her hand.

'There is no pressure, Natasha, let's just see what happens,' he said.

I looked out through the French doors into the garden. It was bathed in a green, underwater light. The day had been tousled and cooler after the storm, branches and leaves strewn across the garden, some pots overturned.

'Shouldn't we wait until later?' I asked.

'It doesn't have to be dark,' he replied, smiling. 'That's only in films.'

'You don't have to do this,' my mother said.

'I want to help find Lewis,' I replied, taking a deep breath.

She raised her eyebrows and took a drink. The clock on the mantelpiece struck eight. Dr Black lit two candles on the table and some incense that smelled of cedar.

'Perhaps you would prefer to leave us, Ms Rothwell?' he said.

She looked unsure briefly and flicked a glance to me. 'I want to stay,' she said firmly and went to sit down beside him.

He looked at her with a mild, polite irritation. 'We must not bring negative energy to the table,' he said seriously, before turning to me. 'There is nothing to be afraid of, Natasha.'

I reluctantly took my place across from Dr Black, who reached out for my hand, and then I closed my eyes.

* * *

It was not Lewis I could see, but Marcus. He was walking in the dark, up the coast path on the Ridge, the one that led to the ledge where we saw the lights. I heard a girl's voice, she was laughing behind him, but he didn't turn. There were shouts and screams in the distance, the trees bent and twisted, a canopy of swaying green above his head.

I opened my eyes slowly, as if waking from a sleep. Dr Black was perfectly still, watching me, his hand still in mine. The room smelled musty and dead, some petals from the flowers on the sideboard had dropped onto the floor and there was a small mound of ash left by the incense on the tablecloth.

I shut my eyes again and took deep breaths. I could hear Dr Black talking softly but could not make out the words. It sounded like a poem or a prayer, there was a rhythm and melody in the rise and fall of his voice. It was soothing and I thought I heard him say Lewis's name. There were other voices too, far away, calling out. I was back in the woods. I saw the blue lights ahead of me in the trees, they winked and sparkled and I understood that they were my guides. The bushes and trees were closer now. I pushed back branches, leaves touched my face and creepers gathered at my feet. I could smell the dank earth and it reminded me of death. The Ridge had always smelled of death and that's what I had never understood before. I also knew I was searching for Marcus, not Lewis.

The phone rang somewhere far away and my mother rose abruptly from the table. I could hear a chair move and the door closing behind her, but I didn't open my eyes. Dr Black touched my hand.

'Stay there,' he whispered.

And his breath was warm on my face, he was close to me.

'Don't come back yet,' he said softly.

I could hear a bird singing somewhere deep in the woods, as if dawn was coming. The light was no longer blue, but grey and empty, as if the colour had drained away. I entered a clearing, and it reminded me of the place Victoria had spoken about, the strange woods in Romania, where the little girl got lost for many years but never aged. The trees were not like the ones on the Ridge, they were bare of all leaves with thin, silvery grey trunks, all gnarled and misshapen, reaching out to touch each other. Marcus was there with the girl, the one from the beach, the girl who went into caves with boys. They were standing facing each other and I knew if I stayed and watched them I would see them touch and become part of each other.

I opened my eyes suddenly. 'Nothing, there is nothing,' I said.

My throat felt scorched, raw, and my chest was heaving.

Dr Black handed me a glass of water. 'You can't say that yet,' he said, eyebrows raised.

I was exhausted and put my head on the table.

'You need to go back,' he said.

'This is too much,' said my mother who must have returned while my eyes were closed. 'She looks unwell, she is so pale.'

'We can't stop now, Ms Rothwell.'

I opened my eyes, the room was shadowy. I looked up and Lewis was standing in the garden watching us. He was leaning against the French doors, dripping wet, his palms upturned on the glass and his eyes wide and sad. 'There, he's there, let him in.' I stood up and pointed frantically at the doors.

The curtains moved and shifted, a crack in the glass letting in a breeze, but neither Dr Black nor my mother could see him.

* * *

She helped me into bed; it was barely nine o'clock, the evening still light outside. I felt exhausted, as if the life had been drained from me. She plumped up the pillows behind me, and left a glass of water on the table beside the bed, pulling over the thin curtains.

'Drink,' she said.

And it was as if I was very small again and off sick from school. The best of days getting to stay home with her; the radio on and her reading beside me or fetching treats and medicine. The feeling that I was getting to see what her day was like when we were apart, a secret world of all her routines and rituals, the sounds of the house when it was just my mother in charge; how it flowed around her.

I couldn't sleep for ages, twisting and turning in the bed, the blankets skewed, the distant sounds of the seafront like an incessant, pulsating beat. People alive elsewhere, far away. A swirling isolation was settling on me and I feared I would forever see Lewis in the window and never anyone else. He would not let me forget my broken promise to protect him.

The lights came back that night, close to midnight, as I finally fell asleep. This time many more people saw them floating above the Ridge; the people who believed and stayed late to worship the stars on the beach; the men and women who didn't believe and drank in the bars along the seafront. The people who had no opinion and liked only to take a walk at night, when the air was cool; the couples who cared only for the flesh of another and hid in the long grass on the path up to the Ridge. All of them saw the lights dance and flicker in the trees, their wavering blue form a rebuke or a revelation depending on where you stood on the matter. Some were filled with awe as they watched, and others with fear.

Whatever your perspective, it had become impossible to deny their existence and in a way whoever you thought you were before they came, mattered little now.

Chapter Twenty-Five

We woke early the next morning to Marcus banging on the front door. My mother pulled back the curtains and opened my bedroom window, sleepy and dishevelled as she leaned out over the ledge.

'The lights, they came back,' he shouted up.

'It's too early,' she called down to him hoarsely.

He sounded excited, curious again, like the way he used to be.

'It's raining,' my mother said mournfully, her hands stretched out into the air.

She started to cry then and her tears were for Lewis, and for me in a way. She could not really hide from the truth of me any more. I would not live as others did and she understood that now. I was marked as the lady in the striped tent on the beach had told us all those years ago.

We didn't say much at breakfast; the night before seemed like a strange, desperate dream. She drank three black coffees, and bit her nails while staring out of the window. Every now and then she looked as if she was about to speak – a question about the seance, and what I had seen, floated in the air between us – but she thought better of it.

'I have to find him, it's all that's left now,' I said.

She drank more coffee and stared out the window. 'I will miss him so, I don't want it to be true,' she said as she got up from the table.

Afterwards I found her kneeling in front of the French doors in the dining room, a hammer and some extra screws in her hand, trying to fix the lock. She then moved some of the lavender pots that lined the path outside and put them leaning on the doors, like a small fortress to ward off unwanted supernatural visitors. The cat watched her with an air of quiet, detached scepticism.

Fear is interesting to observe when you do not feel it yourself. The sense of powerlessness overtaking someone, how it brings forth their most basic and ancient self, which in my mother's case was her deep desire for protection, to lock away the outside, close the shutters and imagine our world could be kept intact, separate and safe from everyone else. She had been preparing for it all our lives in a way. The notion that if we couldn't see them, they could not see us, that by hiding we could escape the censure of strangers and live as we chose. It was a childlike view of things but made sense to her somehow and almost everything about us had been built on this flimsy, flawed structure.

Children and tourists were being interviewed on the TV, the latest sightings were the lead item on the morning news. Lewis had been dislodged. He was always pushed aside. One of the holidaymakers, a fair-haired man, was leaning against the bandstand, a fat baby in his arms. He said he was feeling nervous because no one knew what was going on. The interviewer asked if he thought the town was being contacted by extraterrestrials for a particular reason. He shrugged his shoulders and the baby started to wriggle and cry. I thought how quickly what had once been unimaginable, unintelligible was now discussed as easily as the weather reports. Dr Black had been correct, the lights were like the bright dying gasps of a huge star collapsing into itself, and the star was our own capacity for certainty, our belief in ourselves and the way of things. When it burned, everything that had once seemed impossible, no longer was.

There was the sound of a key in the front door and I turned down the volume on the TV. My mother dropped the hammer or whatever tool she was now using to fortify our windows and rushed out into the hall, her voice light and relieved in its greeting. Mr Bowen was back, with flowers and books. He would care for her. I looked to the TV again. Dr Black was being interviewed now. He was mouthing silent words, his eyes alight with a sense of profound elation and just a hint of wounded justification.

I could hear Mr Bowen's voice in the hall saying, 'It will be OK,' over and over. I laid my head on the table then and started to cry.

* * *

Dr Black called for me at twelve and escorted me to the police station. The seafront was quieter than normal, a light mist had blown in and the air was damp. The Ridge looked lonely, swirled in grey. The amusements were open, though half-empty, some of the men who ran the rides were smoking and chatting. They went silent as we walked past. Marcus's mother watched us from the window of the fish-and-chip shop but there was no sign of Marcus. Victoria was sitting on the steps of the bandstand, her Polaroid camera around her neck. She waved and ran over to me.

'The lights, last night.' She was breathless and pointing at the sky, her china-blue eyes blinking with fear and curiosity. 'They came back,' she said, an urgency in her tone.

She was demanding my full attention, expected it of me. I wanted to say, 'I told you so,' but Dr Black hurried me past her before I could answer. I had been a mere joke yesterday, not worthy of their afternoons playing in the sea. I heard the click of her camera behind me – somewhere there is a fading photo of Dr Black and me walking away.

The usually sleepy Garda station was busy, phones ringing, people talking loudly and the whirr of a fax machine. There was a large poster with Lewis's face on the wall and beside it a map of the area. I recognized the sharp contour of the Ridge and the curve of the beach. There were red pins stuck all over it. Dr Black coughed and tried to get someone's attention; I could feel his irritation at being ignored and he straightened himself up.

'He is dead,' I said to the room.

Everyone went quiet, all eyes were on me. A tall man came out from behind a counter and directed us to a meeting room.

'Lewis is dead,' I said. I felt faint as I spoke the words and had to grip on to a chair.

'Detective Murray.' The man offered me his hand to shake.

He had a thick mop of white hair and large brown eyes. I recognized him from a talk he gave in our school the year before about the dangers of drugs.

'Natasha Rothwell, isn't it?' he said, frowning slightly. 'I've been wanting to talk to you.'

I sat down on the metal chair while Dr Black went to introduce himself.

'I know who you are,' the detective said to me, barely looking at him. 'You live in that lovely old house on the cliffs.' He leaned back in his chair and stared at me.

'Yes,' I said.

'I always think it is a haughty house, part of the town but not,' he said, smiling.

'Have you met my mother?' I asked faintly.

Dr Black smothered a smile.

'I have met her, she came here to talk to me about Lewis and I would feel more comfortable if she was with you now, to be honest, you shouldn't be alone.'

'I didn't tell her I was coming and I didn't know she came here,' I replied.

Dr Black moved to speak but Detective Murray put his hand up to halt him. 'As you have come, I am happy to talk for a short time, but Dr Black, I would ask that you give us a few minutes alone.'

Dr Black looked flushed and hurt but he agreed to leave the room.

'Who is dead?' the detective asked.

'Lewis. He's not coming back.' I rubbed my eyes. I didn't want to cry in front of him.

'We are all very concerned for Lewis's safety. He is a vulnerable young man and has been gone for nearly two weeks, but why do you think he is dead?'

'I saw him. I can see things in dreams, visions, and he was a ghost in our house.' I looked up at him.

Detective Murray sat back in his seat. 'I see,' he said, frowning. 'Thank you for sharing this with us, I know it must be difficult to talk about these experiences. Can I ask you, while you are here, we understand that Lewis was beaten up, attacked in the days leading up to his disappearance, and we believe some of the kids here know more about it than they are willing to admit. Do you know anything about this?'

'They called him a devil,' I said.

Detective Murray sat forward in his seat and his dark eyes were suddenly alert. 'Who called him a devil?'

'I don't know his name, but I can show him to you. There was a group of them, they shouted at him and beat him up last week.'

'Why did they pick on him?'

'Because they thought he was weird, and because of the lights on the Ridge,' I answered.

'When did you last see Lewis?'

'On the beach the night he went missing.'

'Why do you think he is dead? Has someone said something to you about what happened that night?'

'No, I just told you,' I said, wiping my eyes. 'I can feel it, I just explained.'

'Do you know Marcus Whitby well?'

'Yes,' I said, surprised by the question.

'You are friends?' he went on.

'Sort of.'

'Did he tell you something, confess to seeing or knowing something?'

I would have to warn Marcus, tell him the people he had left me for would lead him into trouble. 'No,' I replied.

Detective Murray got up from his seat and poured some water from a jug on a desk in the corner of the room. He offered me some but I shook my head. He took a drink, crumpled the plastic cup and threw it in a bin in the corner of the room. 'You saw the lights also?' he asked.

I nodded and looked down at my hands. They were tanned a very dark brown against the white surface of the table. 'Did you know they came before?' I asked.

He didn't answer for a moment. Then, 'I didn't know that, until recently,' he said, nodding.

'People should listen, take heed, don't you think?' I ask.

'I don't like people in my town to be afraid, whatever the reason,' he said.

'And would you protect me, if I was afraid?' I asked.

'Of course. Are you?' he said. 'Has anyone threatened you in some way?'

'They call me a witch,' I replied.

'I'm sorry, kids can be cruel.'

'I just want to tell the truth, that's why I'm here now. I saw the lights and I wanted to tell people, and now I'm very sure that Lewis is dead. They think the lights are evil, and the lights are what we should be afraid of, but they are just a warning.'

'Thank you, Natasha,' he replied. 'I might need to talk to you again. And please make sure your mother is aware of Dr

Black and all that he is talking to you about. In fact, I will call her myself about it. I understand he is quite controversial, obsessed even with his beliefs.'

I nodded and left the room.

Chapter Twenty-Six

I spent the rest of the afternoon with Dr Black. We walked the Ridge together, trailing through the damp grass and the thin mist that was blowing in off the sea. I brought him to the ledge and showed him where we had seen the lights and then pointed down the side to the rocks below, the place where I felt Lewis had been. It seemed familiar from the seance, though it had been Marcus I had seen there, not him.

'I think perhaps we should try and conduct the seance here this time,' he said, gesturing to the damp ground with a stick he used for walking.

'I don't know whether Detective Murray believes what I told him about Lewis,' I said, sitting on one of the large rocks.

The trees that had been dry and gasping seemed a deeper, dark green, as if their colour and vigour had been restored by the rain of the last few days. The ground too was no longer as scorched, patches of colour returning to the yellow scrub under our feet.

'You can only offer your knowledge, and I expect they are

237

braced for the worst anyway,' he replied, looking out to sea.

'Why do you believe me?' I asked.

'Because I have seen too much not to and you are quite special, you remind me. . .' He stopped.

He leaned against the rock beside me. 'I had a daughter, Florence, but she died when she was only four years old.'

'I'm so sorry. What happened?'

'My wife was driving the car and there was a crash. Florence was killed instantly.'

'That's dreadful,' I said.

'Yes, it was the worst day of my life. One is changed completely after it, which is why I was able to forgive my wife. She left me about a year later for a man who was not worthy of her, I know this as he was my best friend. It was a madness that overtook her. I recognized it as I had it myself. One wanted to smash things, anything to try and forget the past. It seemed strangely appropriate and so I never hated her.'

'Were they happy together?' I asked.

'For a time.'

'Did you hate him?'

'I did, but then not so much.'

'Why do I remind you of Florence?'

'Because in the weeks before she died she drew endless pictures of herself injured and broken. We didn't think anything much of it but then. . . she knew, she foresaw.'

'I'm so sorry,' I said again.

'Well, her loss led me to you, and to all the others. A family who were convinced their dead son talked to them through their radio every evening; the mother of a girl who had predicted a fire in her school and begged not to go, but perished as her mother did not believe her. All of them became my family, the ones who were lying, the ones who were so broken like me by grief and the ones who spoke the truth, who had the gift,' he said.

He pushed himself away from the rock and stood in front of me, looking out again to the sea. 'People are disappointed in me and my views. They do not appreciate the evolution in my thinking and maybe they are correct. If you choose a certain path you must be open to all that accompanies you along it, including disgrace and shame.'

He smiled then. 'I had a patient who claimed to have been abducted by an alien. I was naturally sceptical at first, quite sure he was delusional or suffering from some kind of an illness, but I just couldn't find any evidence for it. I studied and studied him. He was completely normal and well in all respects, except he claimed to have been taken. After that I did more work, more research, met others who had these experiences – ghosts, angels, everything – almost all of them were the same; perfectly rational, sane people who had gone through something extraordinary. It upended my world.'

He looked far away, distracted by memory. 'So I began writing, documenting, interviewing, and it made people,

people I work with, quite uncomfortable. I was embarrassing my employers. They have asked me to take some extended leave,' he finished.

'I'm very glad you are here,' I said. 'I would be completely lost without you.'

And I meant it, for his belief was sort of magnificent, an energy in itself.

'I am writing about you.' He took my hand.

I looked at the large ring on his finger, like something a pope would wear and demand his followers kiss.

'Did you ever try and contact Florence?' I asked.

'Every night for ten years,' he said.

Grief flowed from him suddenly and covered the ground all around us. A black and hateful sadness that had distorted his whole life. Every thought and every feeling had been coloured and it was everywhere, alive in the air, restless, yearning like all the other spirits of the Ridge. The strange mood of the place soaking it up and holding the misery close to its own beating heart somewhere deep in the earth beneath us. I was part of it too.

'Mr Bowen is going to die. That is the connection between him and Lewis,' I blurted out.

He pulled back from me, stood up and leaned more heavily on his stick.

'I tried to tell him, but he doesn't believe me,' I said.

Dr Black took a deep breath. He looked pale and uneasy.

He turned away from me and gazed into the dark, green woods. The breeze was picking up again and the heavy, thick branches moved and swayed.

'You have tried to tell him?' he asked.

'Yes,' I replied.

'You must not speak of this to anyone else,' he said. 'You must focus on Lewis. Do not use your energy for warnings to Mr Bowen that he will never believe. If we can help find Lewis, then everything will follow from that.'

'Perhaps I'm wrong,' I said.

Though I knew that I was not.

* * *

People looked furtive, huddled together as I walked home along the beach in the drizzling summer rain. They were talking about the lights and they didn't find it funny any more. We were being watched from on high, the children who played on the Ridge in danger, our town in the sights of something odd and mysterious. There was to be a prayer service in the church, candles would be lit. Some of the holidaymakers were packing up and returning home early, though the campsites were now overflowing with alien enthusiasts, druids and other curious types from around the country. A few more television crews had arrived, they were standing outside their vans which were parked along the promenade. I spotted Mike in deep conversation with one group, gesturing to the Ridge. Tonight, everyone would be looking to the sky, even Councillor Barry so the rumours went.

'You. . .' an old man shouted at me, his hand raised.

I didn't recognize him but ran the rest of the way along the beach. By the time I reached home it was after seven and dinner was almost ready. Mr Bowen was in the dining room staring out through the French doors and into the garden, where my mother's pots of lavender stood like a small army.

'It's a shame you don't grow garlic, it can ward off evil,' he said without turning.

'The lights came back, when you were away,' I said.

'I know, it's made the news.' He left the window and took his seat at the table.

He was wearing a crisp white shirt that made him look even more tanned, swarthy almost, and his black hair was tousled.

'And ghosts too, apparently.' He reached down to pick up a glass of wine.

I could hear my mother in the kitchen, a cupboard door slamming.

'We loved Lewis,' I said.

'I know, I'm sorry but we don't know anything yet.'

He was so presumptuous and assured that his world view was more complete than mine, than my mother's even. I wondered how she could want to bring that kind of assurance into our lives; we lived in shadows and possibility.

'What were you doing in the city?' I asked.

'Working,' he said, taking a drink.

'Really?'

He didn't answer me but sipped some more. Then, 'Elizabeth is nervous for you,' he said.

'There's nothing new in that.' I walked over to the mantelpiece.

There were some dead flies lying behind one of the pictures. I brushed them off and onto the floor.

'It seems to come with the territory of parenting,' I said. 'Perhaps you already know that?' I turned around to face him.

He looked uncomfortable suddenly, and he pulled at the collar of his perfect white shirt. 'Seances, Ouija boards and the like, it's not good to mess with that stuff.'

My mother entered the room then, carrying a large wooden bowl of salad. She laid it in the centre of the table and stood back as if to admire it. I thought she seemed to be a sort of version of a wife, as she was a version of a mother.

'Mr Bowen was telling me what he was up to in the city,' I said.

She looked at me and a vague flicker of surprise crossed her tired face.

'Not nearly as interesting as what was happening here,' he answered quickly.

She left for the kitchen again and I sat down across from him.

'What is it you want from me?' He sat up straight.

'I'd like you to go home and not come back.'

He sighed and took another drink of his wine. 'I care a lot for your mother,' he replied. Then he paused and looked around him at the table, all set up prettily for three. A new life, a new house, a new family and something like fear, regret even, entered his eyes. 'I would like in time for you to see me as a friend. I'm trying my best despite everything.'

'Friendship requires trust,' I answered.

If he loved my mother should he not have told her he was married, could he not have explained his situation, and asked her to wait?

Afterwards I read his letters to her I understood better. I knew that he didn't tell her about his wife because he didn't know how, he was weak and flawed. And perhaps the vaguely naive, puritanical air that always floated around her made him think she would reject him. The lustful sinner cast out from the austere house that stared at the sea and he could not contemplate that. He perhaps knew too that she was not as bohemian as she pretended. So he paused, tried to hold on to the magic of his summer with her, and sealed his fate.

She re-entered the room then and laid down a plate of cold meats, all arranged in a semicircle with some olives in the middle.

'Dr Black and I will be meeting again later,' I said.

'Why?' she asked.

'I need to find out more about Lewis, I need to contact him.'

'I don't think it's a good idea. You were exhausted, drained last night and it's too strange really, we shouldn't be. . . let the guards work it out.'

'You thought you saw Lewis in the garden the other night, standing on the edge of the orchard,' I answered. 'Did you tell him that?' I gestured to Mr Bowen.

She didn't answer but looked down at her plate.

'Don't pretend to be something you aren't just because he's here,' I said. 'We have a value, without him. We shouldn't have to try and impress him.'

'She did tell me,' he said quietly.

'Natasha, tell Dr Black we do not want him meeting you tonight,' she said firmly.

It seemed an odd moment for her to decide to protect me.

'But I'm trying to find Lewis, don't you want that?' I said.

'Yes, of course, but this is not the way, and we don't know, he could have just gone missing, people do and. . .' She looked away from me to Mr Bowen. She had cried for Lewis this morning, bolted the doors against his ghost. She knew I spoke the truth. Mr Bowen had convinced her otherwise in the intervening hours.

'You thought I was lying about the lights, everyone did, but I wasn't,' I said.

'I don't remember anyone here saying you were lying about the lights,' said Mr Bowen.

I sank into my seat then. 'It felt like that,' I said.

'And we still don't know what they are, it could be a natural phenomenon,' he said.

I sighed heavily.

'Maybe you should not live your life guided entirely by your moods and feelings,' he said.

'That's a very patronizing thing to say and ironic, considering you make up stories for a living,' I answered.

'I know the difference between fact and fiction.'

'Defend me,' I said to my mother.

She shook her head. 'No one is attacking you.' Then, 'Look, Dr Black can come this evening, but this is the last time. I will make sure he understands that.'

'He says I shouldn't change who I am, he understands, he knows other people just like me,' I said.

'Who are you Natasha, who are we really?' she said.

'We were happy, before him,' I replied, looking to Mr Bowen. This was a lie, I knew that even as I spoke the words.

'Mr Bowen. . . Seán and I, we can't pretend any more,' she said.

He looked up surprised, his jaw tight and strained.

'I don't want to pretend any more, he makes me happy.'

'Let's not. . .' he started to say.

She was being too honest, moving too fast for him.

'You have been so difficult this summer,' she said to me, her voice shaking, 'all this trouble and attention seeking. I have tried to be patient, but no more. You are not a child.'

She would abandon her little faith in me for a man who had come to stay for the summer.

'He's married.' I stood up.

'What? Why would you say that? I don't need any more premonitions.' She shook her head, her hand on her neck. She looked to Mr Bowen for comfort, understanding, but he was staring at the table, his hand gripping the wine glass. I wondered if the crystal would shatter under the pressure of his conscience.

'Seán. . .' she started. Her face began to fracture, her lips sank downward, her eyes seemed huge and her brow furrowed and creased. She was distorting, breaking into beautiful little pieces. 'Seán,' she said again.

Her voice spoke of peril, fear, anxiety and also somewhere, deep, deep within, a seed of dark, unwanted knowing, as if she had been built for betrayal, not love. It was a lesson that she had been taught over and over, this was just the latest class.

He didn't answer, couldn't answer, he was unable to raise his head. The silence in the room became unbearable, heavy and overwhelming, as if the ceiling had collapsed in on hope and the possibility of second chances; smashing any belief that your story might not be over, that it might have a different-to-expected ending. Mr Bowen's head stayed bowed as if gravity was forcing him down; his hand clasping, crushing my grandmother's delicate wedding crystal.

Answer her, I thought to myself. Answer her, for she deserves that.

I could not bear to see her so weak, so broken. Perhaps I had cursed her the day he arrived, playing magic with the universe and making her fall in love with him. He was just a paying guest after all, and perhaps he had committed no sin, except to be charming, to be kind, and she was not used to kind men. She read things into it that were perhaps not there. She had nothing to compare the experience to. She lived a sheltered life in a decaying house and never met any interesting or educated people. She thought writing a book meant you were very clever and reading together in the garden meant love. She thought listening meant understanding, she mistook respect, admiration, for something more. He was just a man staying for the summer and enjoying the company of an unexpected beauty.

Mr Bowen could still find no words and the silence was a kind of solemn death.

I walked out of the room and into the garden. The rain had stopped and far out to sea the sky was clearing, a weak evening blue breaking through the heavy grey clouds. I descended the steps, the long grass on either side of me glistened with droplets of moisture. We had all been thirsty for months.

Chapter Twenty-Seven

Victoria's garden was festooned with coloured light bulbs. The front door stood wide open and music was playing somewhere in the house. I stood at the gate for a second and looked over at a long table laid out with giant bowls of food. Wine bottles and glasses were lined up ready for the guests. The starched white tablecloth billowed and rose in the sea breeze. The au pair was sitting on the steps of the house smoking a cigarette. She pointed vaguely to the side garden.

I passed the boat and their large car. It was packed with suitcases, their bikes were attached to the boot, and a canoe was tied to the roof. They were obviously leaving sooner than normal, they never usually held their party this early in August. A smell of smoke came from the side area of the house and there was the sound of people laughing. I recognized Victoria's voice teasing someone. They had lit a small bonfire and were sitting around it toasting marshmallows. Marcus was there, his arm around the cave girl, a bottle of beer between them. Everyone went silent when they saw me, and Marcus slowly stood up.

'Oh, Natasha,' said Victoria. She looked nervous, her eyes darting back and forth to Marcus.

'We're going home tomorrow so we just thought we'd do this thing. . .' she said, gesturing to the group.

'Don't worry, I didn't want an invitation, you don't have to explain,' I said.

Marcus bent down to pick up his beer and whispered something to the girl. I had been going to warn him about Detective Murray but now I felt different.

'Did you see the lights, witch?' one of the boys said.

Marcus took a swig of the beer and shook his head.

'Are they coming to collect you?' said another.

There was laughter and Marcus looked at me with a sort of painful sense of shame.

'Do you want to tell the guards about the mean stuff you did to Lewis?' I addressed the boy. 'Beating him up, scaring him.'

Victoria stretched her legs out and leaned back on her arms, watching me as if it were still all an odd game.

'Chill and have a drink,' someone said.

Another of the boys started to bark like a dog and some of the others laughed. Victoria shushed them with her hand and then looked back to me, her eyes wide with interest and expectation. 'You should stay, we're going to wait up for the lights.' She pointed to the Ridge. 'It's better than being on the beach.'

'It's not a carnival,' I replied.

'It is a bit.' She raised her eyebrows.

'What am I thinking right now?' one of the girls said.

They all started to laugh again, though Victoria didn't, her gaze steady and serious on me.

'Victoria says you can read people's minds?' the girl said.

'Yeah, what am I thinking?' said the boy who had barked.

Everyone laughed again, except Victoria and Marcus – he was rubbing his head and shifting uneasily.

'She's not that pretty, Marcus,' I said.

The cave girl at his feet looked up, alarmed and insulted. She exchanged a shocked glance with one of her friends.

'I mean, all the effort you've gone to this summer, dyeing your hair, getting tattoos, drinking. . . all that, for her,' I said, walking closer to him.

'Don't, Natasha,' he said.

He smelled of cheap aftershave.

'What were you doing at my house this morning, shouting about the lights?' I said.

He shook his head, his cheeks red.

'If you don't care, if you don't believe any more, what are you doing coming to me like that?' I asked.

'I feel sorry for you,' he shouted, his face red.

I shuddered as he said the words but what did I expect really.

'So what, there are lights, it doesn't mean anything,' he said.

The girl at his side on the grass touched his leg and for a second I thought I might need to smack her into oblivion, dislodge her from his side as she had vanished me.

'They will leave you, they always leave,' I said, gesturing to the group. 'They won't remember you come autumn.'

He knew what I meant, there was a flicker of recognition on his face. It was the same every year, people you saw every day, played with on the beach, they left and mostly never came back.

'And Lewis?' I said.

There was not a word from the others, but I saw them exchange nervous glances.

'Stop going on about him, he just fucking ran away. He was always going to do something stupid like that,' said Marcus.

Despite his harsh words, his eyes were sad as he spoke, his discomfort at Lewis's presence still there, it had dogged his childhood. The lost boys. And now his absence was equally troubling, disrupting everyone, making what should have been a summer of sun and wonder into something darker. Maybe it was remorse too, for avoiding him all these years, and now it was too late.

'He was abducted by little green men? Or was it ghosts?' someone said and the laughing started again.

'This is just far too emotional,' said Victoria, lighting a cigarette.

The au pair appeared around the side of the house and

asked us to quieten down, her pretty face irritated and bored at the same time.

'OK, OK,' said Victoria.

'Just go,' said Marcus, sitting back down.

The cave girl stroked his back like she owned him and he shrank into her side.

I never found out her name, I never wanted to know.

* * *

I left Victoria's house and walked the short distance to the Ridge. There was yellow tape across the main path, a lone guard standing watch. Some of the volunteers passed me on their way back from another of their searches. I sat in the long grass and waited, it would be dark soon.

'Have they found out something more about Lewis?' I asked the guard.

He shook his head and gestured for me to move away. I looked back to the beach where a large number of people were gathered in groups, tents set up and bonfires lit all along the edge of the shore. The amusements were running, but deserted, the children had stayed at home or left, the weather and fate of the town uncertain. The giant arm of the Big Dipper reached up high and empty into the murky grey sky, yellow and white lights twinkling all along its underside and reflecting onto the sea below. I looked across to the cliffs at the opposite end of the shoreline and could see the outline of our house. The lights seemed to be blazing in all of the windows. I wondered what Mr Bowen was telling my mother of his life and whether she would believe him.

Close to ten I took the cliff path up the Ridge. Dr Black was to meet me at the summit and I was already late. It was a grey twilight, the evening merging into night and shadows, but every part of the narrow trail was known to me, imprinted on my mind and understood. The turn and dip of the path, the boulders that jutted out and grazed your arms, the gorse that looked like a wall of prickles and fire, impassable except it wasn't, an illusion easily brushed past – a new trail opening up behind. The smells of the shrubbery and feel of the rocks underfoot. I could walk it blind, even now. A landscape that pressed itself to you and shaped your understanding of what it was to move in the world, to navigate a way. Even if you feared it. The rocky parameters of our childhood – Marcus's, Lewis's and mine – dangers and possibilities amidst every crevice. A dream or a nightmare depending on your perspective.

'You have to take it slowly.' Marcus's words to me on the days we took this path; his hand at my shoulder, ready and waiting should I stumble. His breath on my neck. I wiped my eyes, tears at the memory and at the waste, all the time I wasted when I should have told him. We had so many days together, and they had seemed endless but now there were no more. I had lost them both. I was nearing the top, only a few more feet to go. The path narrowed here; I squeezed between two boulders and out into the clearing at the summit.

The sky seemed to explode into endless space and for a second I looked up in wonder and asked the universe to take back all my gifts. I didn't want to understand any more. I didn't want to see what was coming.

Dr Black coughed and I turned. He was sitting on a deck chair in the clearing surrounded by small lanterns and behind him were a group of twenty or thirty people all standing and watching. They seemed to be a mix of ages and I recognized only one, Jim from the caravan park. They looked ghostly in the low light, an unexpected hushed crowd all asking for something, each searching for their own unlikely truth. The knowledge that would change everything and make them somehow understood, all the mysteries laid bare and the world no longer a place without meaning or magic.

'See,' he said, gesturing to the group.

A few smiled and some put their hands together as if they were about to wave, or pray. They were Dr Black's family. All the broken people he had spoken about, who came to him when they saw their lost loved ones on the TV, or blue lights in the sky. I didn't say anything but walked closer to where he was sitting. The candles flickered in the glass at his feet.

'They all believe in you and they have come to witness the lights, with you,' he said. He took my hand then and held it very gently.

'I can't see the lights any more.' I knelt in the dirt.

'Nonsense, you must try. Call them. They will lead us to Lewis.' He reached down to touch my cheeks.

I imagined he saw his daughter, felt her presence when he did that. It wasn't really me at all. I existed for almost no one.

'For Lewis, think of Lewis. He wants you to see them, honour him,' he said.

I stared at him blankly.

There was a hint of alarm in his eyes. 'Do not give up now,' he said.

'I need to go home, my mother, she needs me, and Lewis will be found when he is ready to let us find him,' I said, standing up abruptly.

'Come, come, we must allow the lights to appear,' he breathed heavily.

A few people turned to look into the trees, then whispered to each other before their eyes rested back on me. They had no doubts and it did not make them wise but quite the opposite. To doubt was to live more fully, more freely.

Dr Black rose then and started to speak: '*The lights flickered and darted, deep within the woods ahead, they were beautiful and wondrous, like fairies from a children's tale enticing me along a path to truth.*'

He was quoting the words in my glitter-covered notebook. The group sighed and looked to the sky.

'It's like a rainbow, you never catch it.' I got to my feet and addressed them.

'Maybe they don't want to be understood, maybe there is no meaning, maybe the lights are spirits laughing at us and the mess we have made,' I went on.

There was the screech of a bird high up in the trees above us, and a violent beating of wings in the branches. The people continued to look at me with interest, their eyes wide. They liked my words, believed in them, just at the moment I no longer did.

'You know better than that.' He got up from his chair and spoke loudly now. 'Everything happens for a reason, there is energy everywhere.'

'I don't want to find them any more, I don't want to understand. It is enough to know they exist, we do not have the capacity to understand them,' I said to him.

I turned back towards the cliff edge, but he took my arm gently.

'You don't mean it, you are tired, overwrought,' he said.

'It doesn't matter what they are, they came is what matters – they came before and they will come again,' I said.

'We need to keep going,' he said, his voice urgent and pleading.

And I thought of hope, and joy, love even and all the

impossible things that we chased in the dark. They were not meant to be found, their only purpose was to tantalize and enthral. I thought of my mother crying for Mr Bowen; and the people on the beach, with their alien masks and bonfires to the underworld. What would any of them say or do if they understood what it meant? If they comprehended that we were nothing, that we were small, that we were backwards and primitive. Our lives were inconsequential, and something far more intelligent lurked in the dark of the sky and the gloom of the woods. The message from the lights was about us, about how weak and vulnerable we were, and that we should never forget it.

'You must not give up, we are so close to changing their views, helping them to understand. They won't be able to insult you, insult me, they can't pretend any more that people like us and Lewis don't exist,' he said, holding my hand tightly.

'Lewis,' I said suddenly, shivers running down my arms. My voice echoed through the trees and seemed to rise above and all around us.

Dr Black looked fearful and desperate.

'Lewis,' I called again.

He still held my hand, his eyes bright, desperate for me to deliver something. All of our reputations depending on it.

'You must let me go now,' I said firmly.

The darkness seemed solid, complete, silence all around us. I imagined we were in that strange wood in Romania again, lost here for years. The people who didn't age, trapped in dreams about magical worlds. The real world continuing on without them.

'Lewis is here.' I turned back towards the cliff.

I could feel Lewis's cold breath on my neck, it seemed to be gently pushing me back to the coastal path I had climbed.

The fear left Dr Black's eyes as he watched me and a new game began. I would bring him something other than lights. I would not let him down, I was still part of the family.

'Lewis,' I shouted again.

There was no reply, only the wind moving in the tops of the trees.

'Lewis,' Dr Black called, gesturing to the group.

'Lewis,' they repeated like some kind of a ghostly chorus.

I didn't wait for them, but started to make my way back down the slippery cliff path. He was there, I knew it. He wanted me to find him, to tell my mother. As I scrambled down I heard voices far below on the shore, many of them, the flash of torches and panicked voices rising on the wind. Volunteers in their neon jackets huddled together staring at the sea.

They had found him, washed up in the rockpools.

* * *

There was noise, staring faces, police tape, and the night became bright like day, with floodlights. Detective Murray was there, he would have me escorted home, he said.

'Can I see him?' I pleaded.

He shook his head and I started to shiver uncontrollably. He put a blanket gently around me. 'It's best not to see him, he has been in the water,' he said, leaning down to me.

I pulled away and shouted, 'I need to see him.'

He shook his head again and gestured to one of the women guards to come over. She gently but firmly held my arms and stopped me escaping down to the rocks. A volunteer climbed past shaking his head; he lifted his eyes to me and they were white and haunted.

'He needs me. And you have to tell the people not to touch him, he doesn't like to be touched,' I said.

Detective Murray nodded. 'It's shock, Natasha, it's a terrible shock and I am so sorry.' He spoke softly.

'He needs me and my mother, she will hold him,' I said.

'I know, I know, but he is found and that is what we must be thankful for,' he said. 'He is no longer on his own.'

I turned away from him and behind me Dr Black was deep in conversation with Amy from the TV station. She was fenced off with her crew and some other people who had been on the summit. She caught my eye and stared at me for a minute, before beckoning to me as if we were friends. I had heralded, if not the lights, the presence of a dead boy. The path to renown and recognition was open to me now in a way, but I chose not to follow it.

'You need to go home,' Detective Murray added.

'I should have been able to tell you what happened, I knew he was dead but I didn't know what happened,' I said.

'You did as much as you could,' he answered.

'They think I found him,' I said, pointing to Dr Black and the small band of followers remaining.

'Forget them now. You were here for Lewis tonight,' he whispered.

I was led away from the cliff side and back to the sandy path up the Ridge. I said I could make my way from there and the female guard reluctantly let me go.

There was loud music playing down near the shore, people dancing and shouting, rubbish was blowing along the promenade. I thought about Marcus that night on the Ridge almost a month earlier when he had stayed bent on the ground as the lights shone above us. It had been a choice all along. He had decided not to join me. He wanted something else and I understood it a bit better now. Lewis and I had failed to heed the warnings, despite all my pronouncements.

I passed the train station, and the small private road that led up to Victoria's house. A garda car was parked outside and there was the sound of raised voices from her garden. I could hear the creak of the old garden gate. I ran to the entrance of the train station, deserted now, and peered out from behind one of the pillars. I saw two more guards, they were walking down the laneway and with them was Marcus and one of the other boys, pulling and straining as they went. They steered them to the car and then drove off down the coast road. I leaned against the pillar and took deep breaths, could feel the shivering overtaking me again. Lewis's tattered face fluttered on a poster on the door to the station house, his blank eyes rising and falling in the night breeze, and I started to cry.

Chapter Twenty-Eight

There was a hushed silence when I finally made it home, the house shut in on itself and dark now. There were no records playing softly, no clink of glasses and murmur of voices in the front sitting room. I crept up the stairs, my eyes half-closed for fear of seeing Lewis in the shadows, and dashed into my room. I had barely shut the door when it swung violently open and bounced off the wall. My mother switched on the harsh overhead light. The force of the door opening had left a deep gash in the paintwork behind it. Her face was raw and swollen, her kimono tied unevenly at her waist, and I could smell alcohol on her breath, the edges of her lips stained with red wine.

'Mr Bowen is gone,' she said.

Her eyes were alight with a bright, harsh anger, but underneath there was despair, a haunted, wounded glaze to them. She stumbled out of the room. I closed my eyes shut for a second and thought of a painting in the National Gallery, *The Opening of the Sixth Seal*. My mother and I always made a point of stopping and looking at it, usually the last painting on our annual trail. It was huge and frightening, people cowering as lightning and red fire overtook a craggy valley. Everyone helpless and doomed. We always had tea afterwards to recover. Everything about tonight felt like that forsaken valley.

I went after her and found her lying on her bed, the windows and curtains wide open to the night, the room chilly and damp, a small lamp lit on her bare, unadorned dressing table. The large mahogany wardrobes with the elaborate cornices seemed to lean down over her. She looked tiny and forsaken lying there. I looked at her and I hated Mr Bowen, everything about him. His blue eyes and his calm voice, his books and his ideas, his endlessly rational response to the world, his swimming and his lies. And I wished again, like I had done all that summer, that he had never come.

'They found Lewis,' I said.

She went completely still on the bed.

'He was lying in the water off the Ridge.'

She started to sob then, a lonely wailing that filled the air all around us.

I looked at her sad room, the one without sea views. They were reserved for me and the guests. The furniture in it belonged to all the dead people in the picture frames that lined the walls and it was mostly chipped, or broken, mismatched. She owned almost nothing except her paints and the unfinished canvases. I knew we had little money but why she had so few things remained a mystery. And even now, so many years later, I don't understand. It was as if she barely existed, she was a ghost long before she died, her life filled with vacant and absent spaces, endless silences. She was melancholic and lost before Mr Bowen ever arrived or Lewis died. And to this day I believe, deep within, that the nothingness of her being was all my fault, I was both reason and consequence. I was flame and quencher of her light.

'I wanted to see him, touch him,' I said, shaking.

My mother stopped sobbing and was still again, she would not comfort me and I understood most completely that she could not look after me the way I needed to be looked after, no one ever could.

'But they didn't let me. He had been in the water all this time,' I said.

She covered her head with her hands.

'I wanted to save him, but I didn't. I didn't save anyone,' I went on.

She didn't reply, only turned her back. I switched off the lamp and curled up on the wooden floor beside her bed and stayed there all night.

* * *

The sun came back the next day, the sky a pale, almost translucent blue. The sounds of birds and the seafront were drifting in through the open window of her room. We had slept later than usual, it was almost eleven o'clock. The phone was ringing in the hall below.

I ran down and answered.

'Natasha.' It was Detective Murray. 'I need you to come to the station this morning,' he said.

'I can't,' I answered.

My mother stood dishevelled at the top of the stairs, her eyebrows raised as if to ask whether it was Mr Bowen. I covered the receiver and shook my head. She walked back to her room, and I heard the door close.

'This is not a request,' he said.

* * *

Detective Murray ushered me into the same interview room as before.

'Thank you, Natasha, for coming. Will your mother be joining us?' he asked.

'She can't right now, she is very upset.'

'I would prefer if she was here.' He sat down in the chair opposite me. 'How are you after last night?'

'Lost. I promised I would look after him, save him,' I said, biting my lip.

He reached across the table and gave me a tissue. 'There will be a post-mortem on the body today.'

I nodded.

'We have brought Marcus and one of the other boys in for questioning,' he told me.

'Why?' I asked, rubbing my nose.

'They were involved in a fracas of sorts last night,' he said. 'We also have some new evidence that suggests Lewis may indeed have suffered an injury the night he went missing. A witness has come forward who saw him with the boys. There is no suggestion they killed him, but they may have frightened him and have information as to what happened next.'

I could feel tears in my eyes again and rubbed them harshly, making them sting.

'Marcus wouldn't have hurt him, I know that,' I said.

'The fight last night at the house, it involved you.'

'What do you mean?'

'We understand that things were said about you and Marcus became agitated and hit out.' Detective Murray stood up and leaned against the wall. 'Would you know what that was about?'

'No,' I answered.

He put his hands behind his head for a second and glanced up to the high window. 'We understand that he was defending you.'

The words slid across the table to me. I wanted to take them, cradle them to my chest, cherish them as precious things, but they slipped away, dissolved before their meaning could be held, understood.

'I was there in the garden last night, but only for a short time. There was no fight. They said some things about me, but that's normal,' I said.

He looked at me with pity. 'Marcus and this other boy, they were found to be in possession of some drugs, too.'

'I don't know anything about that. They weren't doing anything when I was there.'

'Thank you, Natasha, for coming here today at such short notice after such a difficult night. If we need anything more we will be in touch,' he finished.

I stood up and opened the door.

'There will be a lot of rumour and misinformation over the coming weeks and months,' he said. 'I think it best if you stay out of the debate. For your own safety, and also for Lewis's sake. We need to understand what happened to him.'

I turned back into the white, bright room. 'You're leaving,' I said.

'What?' He sat up straighter.

'You are going somewhere else, somewhere new.'

'Aren't we all in a way?' He smiled uncomfortably.

'I'm not,' I answered.

Marcus's mother was in the waiting room as I left. She

was pale, alone, clutching a coffee cup, and didn't even glance up as I passed. Outside, their shop was shuttered, the bin beside the door overflowing, and the sign on the door read *Closed*.

Chapter Twenty-Nine

The first of Mr Bowen's letters arrived that evening. He must have written and posted it on his way home the previous night. There was an urgency visible in the tight, black handwriting. It was marked *Private and Confidential*. I placed the cream envelope on the kitchen table. My mother wandered into the kitchen close to eight o'clock, and, noticing the letter, stared at it for a few seconds, before storing it with the bills and junk mail we always meant to go through but never did.

I made the meal and we ate quietly at the kitchen table, the window open. The evening was warm, the garden bathed in golden sun, like summer returned, and the sky was blue and pink. The cat was rolling in the long grass at the entrance to the orchard, moths darting above her in the shade of the trees. My mother didn't finish her food, pushing the plate away and retrieving an open bottle of rosé wine from the fridge. She sat down and drank quickly from her glass.

'I need to find that picture, the one I did of Lewis's

parents when they were married,' she said, 'and the sketches I did of him. I want to give them to her.'

She drank some more wine and looked out the window. 'I can't believe he won't be here again. I can never believe that, when someone dies, that they won't be back. It just seems so unbelievable, impossible,' she said, wiping her eye. 'Was it an accident, do they know yet?' she said.

'They don't know. I think he was afraid of the lights and he panicked,' I said.

I had felt no violence around him, he had been lured away – not by the boys.

'He deserved so much better. He was such a pure soul and he understood far more than people knew, and he had so much sadness in his life, his father and. . .'

I had made her some coffee and left it on the table in front of her. She looked at the mug, her eyes closed off from me.

'Nothing is fair,' I said.

'Why did you tell me?' she said suddenly, her green eyes wide.

Mr Bowen drifted across my eyeline, he would never really leave us. 'Because he was lying and betraying you,' I replied.

'You always want to be the hero,' she said.

It was what Marcus had said to me on the rocks all those weeks earlier.

'He was pretending,' I answered.

'I am most grateful, you saved me from a moral disaster.' She had turned her head to the window and the garden beyond. 'It is so useful having a psychic for a daughter. No need to make my own mistakes, no need to live, to fail on one's own terms. You have the blueprint for everything already. Up here.' She pointed to her temple.

'Well, forgive him, take him back,' I said.

She slumped in her seat. 'Maybe I shall.'

'Then read his letter.' I got up and retrieved it from the pile and threw it across the table to her.

She deflated then in the chair, regret on her face. 'I'm sorry.' She shook her head, looked at the letter again, then pushed her chair back and went to the sitting room.

I cleared the plates away and filled the sink with hot water. I noticed yesterday's local newspaper folded up on the counter. There was another article about the lights by Mike Ryan. This time it featured a blurry photograph that claimed to have captured the floating orbs over the Ridge. A scientist explained it away as dust, and claimed the lights might have been the refracted reflections of street lights or from the amusements. Councillor Barry was quoted as saying he had asked the National Metrological Institute to investigate the matter. The rest of the piece focused on the rise in antisocial behaviour that had accompanied the sightings over the course of the summer. It had attracted all types apparently, pushed out the God-fearing families and welcomed in the pagans.

There was banging on the front door. I opened it and Marcus was there, wearing the same clothes as he had been the previous night. His arms were covered in bruises, and there was a cut on his cheek.

'You're a liar,' shouted Marcus to my face.

I was about to answer, when he pushed the door inwards and forced himself into the hallway, placing his weight against the door. He stood tall over me, his eyes a thin sliver of light blue.

My mother appeared at the entrance to the sitting room. 'Marcus,' she said firmly.

He appealed to her over my shoulder. 'She lied about me, they think I hurt Lewis.'

'I didn't say anything to them, I told them it was an accident,' I said.

'Marcus, you need to go home,' said my mother. 'It won't help anything, only get you into more trouble.'

'I didn't, Marcus, I swear, please believe me.' I reached out to touch him.

He shoved me away and I noticed he was wearing his father's bracelet again. His wrist was red around the edges of it, as if it had been pressed against his skin and held there.

'Marcus, if you have nothing to hide about Lewis, you will be OK,' my mother said. She left us then and went back to the sitting room.

Marcus watched her go. His hands were shaking and his

lower lip was protruding. 'You are such a jealous bitch,' he said, shaking his head. 'I defended you.' He rubbed his forehead over and over as if he had the worst of headaches.

'I lost friends over you, things people said on the bus home from school. They called your mother a whore, and you a bastard. I used to fight them. I told them your mother was a lady and that you were special,' he said.

'No, you didn't, no you didn't.' I started to cry. 'Why did you like her, and not me?'

'What?' he said.

'You touched her, the way you never touched me,' I said.

He flushed and looked over at his hand that was still pressing the door open, the bracelet cutting into his skin from the force of his weight. 'That's nothing now,' he said.

'She's gone, hasn't she? The way they always go.'

He looked back at me, his stare bruised and sad. He was as alone and abandoned as I was, and would always be dogged by rumours that he had something to do with Lewis's death in that strange summer.

'I didn't lie, I never once lied about you,' I said, pleading with him.

'I don't believe you, I don't believe you any more. What happened with the end-of-the-world crap? You were scaring everyone,' he said.

'It was the end of the world. Look at us, look at Lewis. Everything is gone.'

His anger seemed to dissipate then, and exhaustion overwhelmed him. He leaned heavily against the door.

'Did you love her?' I asked.

He shook his head as if he was weary, as weary as anyone could possibly be.

'I didn't need to,' he said, rubbing his head against his outstretched arm.

And I understood what he meant, and I didn't need to think about her ever again after that, which gave me a sort of forlorn consolation.

'I would never lie about you, I told the detective you would never hurt anyone, you have to believe me. And I promise, I'm going to change. I'm not doing this any more. I'm going to pretend I don't hear the voices, or see anything in dreams. I'm not going to try and save anyone. I will be better, better than I was. I am going to change for you and for my mother, because it's made you both unhappy. I can hide, I can pretend again. I can be normal, like other girls,' I said, wiping tears away.

He just shook his head and then kicked the door hard. There was a limit to words, they took you only so far.

'It was too much, Sasha. What were you even doing going to the guards?' he said, shaking his head again.

Sasha was the name he had used to call me, when we first met and had played in the garden. He hadn't used that name in so many years and to hear it again was like catching a lost childhood melody.

'This summer, everything. . . I just couldn't any more,' he said.

He turned suddenly then and walked out of the house and down the gravel path, his head bowed and his hands in his pockets. I slid down the wall of the hall and, lying to myself, said over and over, I will never miss you and I don't care what happens to you. But even as I spoke the words, something in my head kept saying, he will come back. He will come back because we share an essence, and without me he won't really be whole, ever.

I was wrong, though, he never came back.

Chapter Thirty

Mr Bowen's letters kept coming, she lined them up on the hall table, one for almost every day of August, and most evenings at seven the phone would ring. We presumed it was him. My mother and I would invariably be sitting in the garden, plates of salad on our knees, wine at her feet and the hall door open, when it would begin ringing. The silence between us and the shrill call of the phone forever entwined with the dying days of that summer.

She was withdrawn still, ate little, slept late most mornings and forgot to shop. I rang the local grocery store to arrange for a weekly delivery, I could not face leaving the house either. We didn't even go to Lewis's funeral. We got dressed to go, stood at the gate of the garden but couldn't make it down the steps. Days of guilt and shame followed this decision, my mother barely leaving her room. I wrote to Lewis's mother and tried to explain, the ink smudged, and then failed to post the letter as it involved leaving the house. It too rested on the hall table.

It was a return to our life before, though more extreme, lonelier with a greater air of neglect. The bedrooms on the second floor untidy, stuffy, windows unopened, dust on all the surfaces; the garden too was growing wild, the lawn uncut and weeds in the gravel. My mother cared only for the fruit ripening in the orchard, she checked and tended this summer's crop with care and interest. I waited for Marcus to call but he never did. Detective Murray did, however. The post-mortem revealed that Lewis had drowned, his injuries were consistent with a fall and almost three weeks lost in the water. The boys were exonerated, free to move on, and away into the future.

'I'm going to another station,' he said.

'Good luck,' I answered.

'You can probably tell how it will work out,' he said, and I knew from his voice that he was smiling.

Dr Black called in later that week. I had not seen him since the night Lewis was found below the Ridge. I could feel my mother stiffen. She gave him a vague hello and disappeared into the orchard.

'I am leaving.' He sat down on the wrought-iron chair.

'When will you be back?' I asked.

'I won't.' He turned to me and rested his hat on the table beside him. I understood enough not to ask any further questions. Disappointment hung in the air. My 'finding' Lewis had not been enough to convince people of much. You were either the type of person who believed or you weren't, and the preaching of one girl was not going to change that, and the lights had gone away.

He rummaged in his bag and took out my notebook.

'An impressive record of accurate predictions, Ms Rothwell,' he said, handing it to me.

I was distracted again by the childish glitter and the doodles on the cover. It looked like a book from a different part of my life, something to be packed away now.

'You must not underestimate, or give up on, your gift,' he said.

'I won't keep a record any more,' I replied.

'Why ever not?'

'It made everyone unhappy and served absolutely no purpose. Besides, the visions that matter, you don't need to write down, they never leave, even if you want them to.'

He sighed heavily and looked out to the coast. 'You were missed at Lewis's funeral,' he said, looking at me sideways.

'We were too sad to go.'

'I can understand that.'

'What happened to the people on the Ridge that night?' I asked.

'They think you are quite magnificent.'

'But what I said about the lights?'

'They know the hero must always, always reject his or her calling first. It makes you more believable if anything.'

It was ironic.

He smiled then and turned back to face me. 'You must see yourself as a pilgrim, a pioneer.'

'Why did Lewis have to die?' I asked.

'Even I can't answer that,' he replied.

'But the lights, why did they drive him away?'

'It was a warning, as you predicted all along,' he replied.

'But it shouldn't have been him.'

'Somebody has to die, isn't that the rule? Like my little Florence.'

The cat wandered slowly past, ears alert and back arched.

'The lights will return, and you will see them again, you know that. You can't run from your fate,' he said.

'You can run from it for a while, that's what I'm going to do from now on,' I replied.

I imagined my future as a blank nothingness; I would practise forgetting.

'I will still be writing about you,' he said. 'I will be in touch, this is not the end.'

'Will you go back to the hospital?' I asked.

'There is a tribunal of sorts in October that I will be required to attend.'

'But will you teach again?' I asked.

'Yes, if they find in my favour,' he replied.

'What do you mean?'

'If they see fit to judge my research as worthy, and not an embarrassment.'

'I told you everyone tests everyone else,' I said.

'Perhaps. I think you certainly passed the test with Detective Murray and the people on the Ridge that night,' he said, smiling.

'I could tell fortunes for a living when I'm older, set up a tent on the beach, if all else fails.'

'That would be a cheapening. . .' He turned back to look up at the house.

'I have dreamed about Lewis,' I said.

Dr Black sat up straight and clenched his fists, his ring glinted and sparkled in the sun. 'And what did you see?' he asked.

'He is wandering here in the garden, always here. He seems happy and not lost at all. I thought he would be angry with me, or even sad but he isn't,' I said.

'He is at rest,' he replied.

'I'm sorry that I couldn't see the lights that night on the Ridge. I didn't want to any more.'

'They have not been seen this week. They have vanished again. You felt Lewis, though, and for that you will be remembered, by a few anyway.'

We stayed in silence for a minute, the garden a haze of golden light and moths.

He looked at me, I could feel his gaze on my profile. 'Where is Mr Bowen these days?' he asked.

'He left. He lied to my mother, I had to tell her.'

'So it was not an actual death then,' he said, watching me closely.

I shrugged my shoulders.

'She liked him very much, I believe,' he said.

'He was untrustworthy, she can do far better than him, if she wants.'

'But she may not want another, and I'm sure you might object if she found someone else,' he replied.

I felt affronted and we slipped into silence again.

He eventually picked up his hat and offered his hand. 'I hope we can stay in touch,' he said.

'I'd like that.'

'I envy you,' he said, standing up. 'I still live in a world of dualities. You've transcended all that.'

'It doesn't feel like that. I am quite earthbound, I can assure you,' I said.

'Isn't that always the way?' He smiled sadly.

'Satis house.' He gestured to the brambles that grew wild and thick under the windows. 'You will be completely covered over soon, encased.'

'What does "satis" mean?' I asked.

He walked casually to the gate then, casting a last glance towards the orchard, where my mother's humming could still be heard in the warm, still air. 'Ask your lovely mother, she will know Dickens I feel sure... and please do give her my very best regards. I have intruded on your summer.'

His voice blew away down the cliffs and he disappeared from sight.

We never did stay in touch and he didn't fare well at the tribunal. The hospital committee described him and his work as 'professionally irresponsible'. We read about it in the paper. He didn't lose his job then, that came about a year later when his book about my visions and the lights was published. He was deemed to have crossed the line completely, with someone even calling him a cult leader. I went to a bookshop in the city to buy a copy, our library wouldn't stock it. Everyone in the town was embarrassed about that summer. I traced the references at the back for my name. I appeared on several pages. He described me as pure, without pathologies, and my experiences as 'unaccountable in the material world'. I liked that phrase. He was cruel about the town, however, described it as a place of souvenirs and warm beer.

It didn't disappear though, his book, it attained a sort of strange cult status, as did the town. For years afterwards people would make day trips to the Ridge. There was even a haunted camping tour, where a guide would take people to stay there overnight. I heard they wore T-shirts with Lewis's face printed on them. Some believed he had been abducted by aliens then dropped back to earth, his body breaking on the stony shore; others that the restless spirits of the people who killed themselves on the Ridge had tempted him over the cliffs.

We had moved away by then, though, so perhaps this is an exaggeration.

But it did hang over us, all of us who were there that summer. If someone asked where you were from and you answered honestly, they would all recognize the name. The place that was visited by weird lights; the lost boy stolen away in the night and discarded, unwanted. The parties on the beach, the orgies on the Ridge, the crazed young people attacking each other, the drugs and the tales of evil things in the shadows. We were all part of an intense display of human oddity, splendour, decay, and people remembered it – the summer reality paused and folklore took over. We never really escaped it, no matter how far away we went.

And Dr Black was right, I did see the lights again many times, in many places, though I never told anyone about it. And each time they came I knew I would soon lose something or someone important to me.

Chapter Thirty-One

Everyone was gone now, the house quiet, the garden wild, drenched in sunlight by day and rainstorms by night. The fruit was almost ready for harvest, the exceptional heat of July had propelled its growth and red apples hung heavy from the low branches. My mother left a wicker basket on the floor of the kitchen, while the Kilner jars were sterilized and lined up on the dresser. The season of stewing and pickling was just around the corner. I wondered whether she would buy me a new school bag this year. I imagined not, though, as Mr Bowen leaving early had left us with even less money than usual.

His letters were piled high on the hall table, almost twenty of them in total now, neat cream envelopes filled with what gestures of love or requests for forgiveness I didn't know about until much later. They disappeared one afternoon, only an outline of dust remained. She was reading them quietly and allowing him back into her soul.

I woke most nights to heavy rain against the window, the room cooler and more comfortable than earlier in the summer.

The dolls would be staring down at me from the shelf, perhaps wondering what had happened to the fair-haired boy who used to visit. I felt nothing of Marcus's thoughts, his feelings. There had been a time when I could tell his mood without seeing him, but not any more. The psychic bond had been broken, not by me, but by him. Marcus had vacated me and an absence that would never be filled was left behind.

I would leave my bedroom door open and most nights I could hear the rise and fall of my mother's breathing. Her light left burning until late. She dreamed violently some nights, and she sleep-talked sometimes too – mumbles and cries that offered no sense. I would ask her over breakfast in the morning how she had slept, and she would always say the same thing – perfectly fine. She either didn't remember or didn't want to tell me what was haunting her, though I could guess. I tidied her room most days, picking up the clothes she had strewn and collecting the cups and glasses she left on the bedside table. One day I noticed Mr Bowen's novel lying in the unmade covers of the bed. I could not bring myself to pick it up. It was unnerving that even at this distance, like with the letters, his liquid words could find their way to her.

My sleep was mostly undisturbed, there were no more visions of Lewis, or the town drowning in water, under dancing blue lights. My mind was emptied, drained of all knowledge or expectation. I was living in the endless everyday and I thought perhaps I could exist as others did, a blind version of myself, the third eye gouged out. I was not Lewis, I was well and I could save myself and my mother. Her depressions, her despair, the lostness of her existence might recede if she thought I was no longer able to see the future. I could join a tennis club and make amends. I would try harder at school this year, I would make some friends and not tell them anything about their fate.

I would forgive my mother for not being able to ever talk to me about it all.

A new energy came over me for a few days. I aired the empty bedrooms and dusted away the flies that lay in the corners of the hot, dead rooms. I would show her things I had done and attempt to get her approval, which she invariably withheld. I tidied the kitchen and thought about returning to the town, but I only made it to the cliff steps. I was not ready for that yet. I stood in the long grass and stared down. The seafront was quieter, most of the cars on the coast road driving away, back to the city. The amusements empty and ready to be packed up. When I turned back, my mother was standing on the path watching. She was wearing her long cream dress, the skirt of which blew gently around her, and she seemed like a bride. The grasses and the wildflowers her bouquet, her silent gaze an impenetrable veil.

I set up her canvas and paints in the garden.

'Look,' I said.

'Thank you,' she replied.

But she wandered back into the cool, dark of the house.

School was starting in two days. I dug out my uniform and ironed the white shirt that was now an off-white colour and not at all presentable. She steeped it in a bucket of bleach in the garden and we both stared wordlessly at the submerged garment for a minute. I packed my old school bag and left it at the door in the hall, a statement of intent, of hope for better times. I kept busy warding off any visions or thoughts, and every time I had the familiar sense of something or someone trying to reach for me, I would shut my eyes and cover my ears. I did not want to let them in any more, they would have to find someone else.

There is of course no escape from the self, for any of us. I woke the last night of August with the most terrible fever, freezing cold one minute and sweating the next. I lay in the narrow bed shaking with both heat and fear, a heavy weight on my chest, bearing down on me and making it hard to breathe. The house seemed to be moving, swaying, and I imagined it had come away from the cliffs and was unmoored, floating out to the dark sea. I called out, but my mother didn't come. I could hear her sleeping soundly and if she heard me in her dreams she chose not to rise.

I went back to sleep and had the most vivid of all the dreams in which Mr Bowen featured. He was sitting in the garden at twilight, the letters he had sent to my mother stacked neatly on his lap. The sky above the house was a very pale pink and bats darted high over our heads. The garden was a lush jungle of dark shapes and contours, the air alive with moths and the sweet scent of honeysuckle that trailed up the gable end of the house. Grass yellowing and overgrown moved gently in the breeze, and the marmalade cat lay asleep in the shadows. My mother was picking fruit in the orchard. I could hear her singing in the distance and imagined her with a basket on a brown arm, wandering under heavy trees, barefoot and distracted in the long, damp grass.

I went to Mr Bowen in his chair and found him crying quietly into his hands. There were tear stains on the envelopes. He couldn't bring himself to look up and he shuddered at my presence. I stood close beside him and felt his despair, an emptiness that could pierce through you, a sense of unfathomable loss overwhelming him. I noticed the suitcase at his feet, his belongings tidied away, strapped up in old battered leather. He looked up at me then, his blue eyes red and streaming, the sadness in his soul brimming up. His face was no longer handsome but bloated and misshapen. He tried to offer me the letters, the story of his life, his pleas for forgiveness and understanding – take them. He mouthed the words and his arms were outstretched, pleading. I refused though, shaking my head firmly to make sure he understood, for it was too late. He bowed slowly, finally, and iced water gushed out of him in a rush of blue, flowing onto the grass, covering the entire garden, slipping over the gate and down the cliffs to the sea below.

The next morning I woke late to what sounded like Mr Bowen's cool, calm voice in the kitchen below. Drained and exhausted, I attempted to sit up but collapsed against the pillows. I assured myself it was all in my imagination and went back to sleep. He could not have returned.

* * *

I crept down the stairs late that afternoon, sun streaming in through the open front door and the last of the summer roses in a bowl on the hall table. The house was empty, so I went out into the garden. The cat lay under the trees at the entrance to the orchard. She raised her head when she saw me, her ears pricked up and alert, her tail like a question mark; a warning, curled in the air.

I heard him speaking in the distance, caught a glimpse of his dark head. They were under the low trees. They couldn't see me, I was nothing but a shadow, concealed in the rich, green foliage beneath an orange sun. The air was filled with the sweetness of ripe apples and wet earth, and she was laughing and all that was dark in her had gone away again, the poison removed. My body was weak from fever and thirst and I was unsteady on my feet so I left them to their reunion and beat a faltering, diminished retreat to my room.

'And what did you feel when you saw him?' my therapist asks me now, so many years later.

'That some things are inevitable, and you may be able to see the future, but you cannot really change it,' I reply.

She chewed on her pen as I spoke. I remained an enigma to her in the end too.

My mother visited me in my bedroom later, when the sun had gone down and an east wind had whipped up, the weather changing again. The windows in my room rattled and creaked with the strain, the attic groaned and stirred above my head, the light in the hall below flickered in the gloom of a now dull evening. The house was rejecting him, as I had done. She fed me chicken soup in a cup, and lifted a sweet drink to my dry, parched lips. She fixed my bedcovers and closed the curtains to the night, all her energy and life force returned. He gave her something to live for, in a way I never could.

She wiped my brow and told me he had chosen us, and she had forgiven him. And we must ask no more questions, not of the past nor of the future – the answer to everything an averted gaze.

We were a family now and it was time for sleep.

SEPTEMBER

Chapter Thirty-Two

Mr Bowen went swimming the next morning as if nothing had changed. We had yet to speak so I watched him from my room, the towel thrown over his shoulder, whistling a tune as he walked through the garden. I had not heard him do that before. The wind that had blown up overnight had ripped the leaves from the trees. They lay strewn across the garden, and in the distance the sea was steel grey and high, rippled with white foam. I pulled the window open, just as he disappeared down the steps. The air was sharp and fresh, there was a thick dew on the grass and a lone magpie was pecking the apples that last night's wind had shaken onto the gravel path.

I descended the stairs and could hear my mother in the kitchen, the radio on and the kettle whistling, smell the aroma of apples stewing in the air. I stood outside the door for a second, and I thought about warning her how the man she loved would not be coming back. She had wasted her forgiveness. I had seen it all, in many dreams, and the day had finally come.

'Feeling better?' she called out. She pulled open the door

to see me more clearly. Then, 'Don't,' she said suddenly, and she held her hand up as if to ward me off and all the other evil spirits of the world.

My face had obviously not yet learned to live by the new rules, it still spoke of portents of doom. I would have to learn to train it better, to reign in its prophecies. I didn't answer her and walked away.

Would she have listened to me? My therapist dwells on this question, she sees it as the key to unlocking my life ever since and perhaps she is correct. I have learned that people don't really want to know the truth. They think they do, but they don't really, and maybe they are right in the end. It is easier to laugh, or fear, than it is to understand, and ignorance can be a sort of comfort. Besides, I was tainted so she would not have heard me anyway. It was likely another of my strange premonitions, they might be true, or they might not. This is what I have told myself ever since, anyway. It provides a weak form of absolution.

I walked out the front door to the gate at the edge of the garden and looked down the cliffs. Mr Bowen had crossed the road towards the seafront, his towel under his arm now. His strides were long and straight as they had been that first day, a lifetime ago, when the summer seemed endless. I heard crashing from the house behind me, and my mother flitted across the window. Something had fallen, something else she had neglected to give her attention to until it was too late. I felt sorry for her and the mess she had made of her life, of our lives, and I thought maybe I should stop it all from happening. Perhaps I could make him leave the beach, go without the sea today and offer him as a gift to her. The man I saved from his own fate, not because I valued him, but because I valued her. She would have to love me completely then, every part of me, including my dark, third eye.

I walked slowly down the steps. The grass was high and feathery, blowing in the cool breeze, and the sky was a charcoal grey now, clouds gathering over the ocean. I could hear the roar and screech of a train as it entered the tunnel, before rounding the last bend of the cliffs and reaching the station. Mr Bowen was in the distance, he had slowed and was walking at a more leisurely pace, turning his head from side to side as if drinking in the sights of the town as the season turned, ever curious and enamoured with the fading glamour of the place. He waved at someone jogging past.

He felt at home here, and maybe he could have been our bridge to greater acceptance. People had time for him; even though he had run away from his wife, they would have forgiven him. His easy manner and slow smile would have brought them round. He might have coaxed my mother out into the world, let her stand tall in the sunshine and helped her to stop feeling ashamed. They would have been spoken about as star-crossed lovers, who gave up everything for each other, like an ageing Romeo and Juliet. The proof that soulmates exist and love could come calling, even when you were getting old and had made many mistakes.

He walked on ahead of me. I could catch up with him, call his name and let him die another day. He was not a bad man, he was never a bad man, just trapped in a life he didn't want any more and an interruption to mine. He had even tried to like me at first, had made an effort, but it would never have been possible. My need for her love was far greater than his desire, and besides, I had promised myself not to interfere with the future any more. It was my unspoken pledge to her, and Marcus.

He passed the bandstand, the promenade was almost empty, the amusements packed up and gone. The houses on the seafront had their doors and windows wide open, being aired and cleaned. Some of the shops had their shutters up. Everything had been sold or tidied away. It was like an act of abandonment when the tourists left, all the diversions they'd promised passed with the shortening of the evenings and the fall of the fruit. It was one of the lessons of growing up here – people came and then they went. Nothing much lasted, not the weather nor the people you thought you had come to know. Everything was just a day away from being a memory, or something you had to forget. Mr Bowen did not seem to be aware of that.

I pushed through the gate onto the road and followed in his footsteps towards the promenade. The train had arrived in the station, the doors were open but no one alighted and there was a smell of diesel in the air. Large white birds blown in from the coast flew over me in a rush of wings and speeding air. He had reached the beach now and was walking to the edge of the shore. He stopped to pick something up. I watched him lay his towel down, stretch his arms wide, and for a second he just stood staring at the wild and magnificent sea.

What was he thinking? Could he not see the strength of the waves that day, their blind and uncaring force, their pitiless judgement of the brave fools who dared to swim out? He must have believed he could conquer things, as he did my mother. It was perhaps why he wrote about the past, stories of men who changed the world with the strength of their will, who broke the rules and followed their hearts. He liked the heroism of great men but also the sad things that befell them. There was a natural melancholy in him, as there was in my mother, and he recognized it, maybe even more than her beauty. He tried to rescue her, though his life was a mess too, yet still he came with his suitcase and his kind words and thought he had something to offer us. The self-belief of even the humblest of men. But perhaps that is harsh, and it was the power of hope instead. A man who despite everything had hope that at this stage in his life he could turn things around, change them. He just had to be brave enough. The summer had been a test for him, too.

He skimmed a pebble across the waves; a dog ran along the water's edge and he followed it with his eyes, his head turned to watch as it ran up the beach. I started to walk faster now, past the bandstand. An elderly couple linking arms and leaning on a cane walked towards me, their heads down. I descended the sandy steps to the beach. Mr Bowen was entering the water and he seemed to give off a blazing white light in the grey of the morning. His body strong and taut, alive. I glanced to the Ridge briefly. There was a faint line of smoke; I breathed in to see if the wind had carried it to the beach but there was only the smell of seaweed and fresh, fresh air. When I turned back to the ocean Mr Bowen had submerged himself, his head appearing then from under the large, white waves, black and free, tossed from side to side.

* * *

She told me once that they had felt happy and sad about the same things and that for her was love. She had been drinking wine when she spoke which might explain the simplicity of the phrase and indeed its openness, but it was strangely moving. It could have been a description of friendship also, and maybe that was a form of pale love. Marcus and I had been the same, we had felt strongly about the same things until we didn't, and it had seemed like a very great betrayal, one that had burned me inside and made me view things differently. I should have told her neither of us was made for connecting with people, it required a capacity for openness and depth of heart that we both lacked. It was such an act of daring to think you might enter the life of another, invade them with your desire and your visions of an imagined future. I didn't think either of us had the strength of will for the action required and certainly not the energy to sustain it.

What happens to the things we don't complete? The stories we never finish, the passions we feel sure are everything, but that come to nothing? Dr Black said there was another parallel world, where those other 'might have been' lives go on. The lives we expected to have, even deserved. And this universe could run in tandem with ours but we just weren't able to see it, a thin veil separating who we were from who we might have been. There might have been a beautiful me somewhere else with lots of friends, a father, a world where my mother was happy and I didn't try to save people, because they didn't really want it.

A life where I don't to this day feel the invading thoughts of others as we stand in a queue for coffee; where I don't see lonely, lost souls in the shadows; where I do not already know how it will end for you, even though we have just met. A life where my mother didn't die young and leave me alone in the city, with no house, no father and a dubious past. A life where that summer didn't drown us all in its heat and strangeness, where Lewis lived and Marcus didn't hate me and refuse to speak to me ever again. My letters returned with black marker covering every line, and then only an eternal silence.

He went to college and became, of all things, a social worker. I know this because I saw him once in the hospital. It was close to the end for my mother, endless days spent in a waiting room, or sitting by her bed. The sounds of the world going on without us outside the window. I saw him down the corridor, a file under his arm, talking to an old man. He looked quite beautiful, tall and fair but cleaned up and accomplished; an air of deep respect in his mannerisms and gestures to this elderly man.

And I thought of that afternoon when we were twelve and I had told him about my visions. He had listened, his eyes wide, and afterwards he had held my hand. I never again had a friend like him, and I couldn't remember sometimes what went wrong. I didn't know why I wasn't good enough and whether it was my fault or his, and why things had to change. It was the thing I feared the most. Not lights in the sky, nor ghosts in my room, not death even, but change, the upending of my world and the passions that came with it. I have been helped to understand this fact over the years. My mother falling in love, Marcus growing up. It was they who were becoming that summer, not me. I was left far behind.

I watched Marcus for a few minutes that day in the hospital, willing him to look down the corridor and see me, but he didn't glance my way and eventually walked in the opposite direction, his hand on the man's back guiding him out. The nurse who had noticed me watching assured me he was 'a great guy', her eyes filled with longing as he walked away. And I remembered the feel of his head against my shoulder, his tears in the dark, and I thought, why didn't I let you kiss me that night on the Ridge? It might have meant something. I might have had the other possible life, the one that existed only in Dr Black's strange, alternate universe. And even if it hadn't changed things it would have happened and I would not have imagined it and somewhere, somewhere deep in his memory there would be a kiss, instead of an accusation that I didn't even make. At the very least I would have liked to tell him that I didn't try to save people any more, starting the day Mr Bowen swam out into an autumn swell. I lied instead now, and tried not to scare people with the truth about who both they, and I, actually were. I pretended not to see a single thing.

'When Elizabeth Rothwell dies, please make sure to tell him,' I said to the nurse, tears on my cheeks.

I don't know if she ever did, but he never tried to find me.

* * *

Mr Bowen swam on, further and further out. The sky darkened, and I felt the first of the rain. I raised my head. It was light and gentle on my skin but there was a quiet persistence to it, more than a shower. I looked at my legs, the tan pale in the grey light; my brown legs would fade to white soon and truly then nothing of the summer would remain. School next week, where people would talk about me behind their hands. My mother meanwhile would try again to fit in with the other parents but wouldn't really, though people would make an effort because despite everything, she was a lady with an air of another, older world about her. And she had a lovely face.

Mr Bowen told me once he had won medals for swimming. I imagined him standing on a podium somewhere as a young boy, his flushed pride at the claps of the crowd and a heavy medallion around his thin neck. His mother in her flowery dress waving him on from the sandy beach. Her serious boy with the straight, careful stare who tried his best and worked hard at the things he believed in. Could I have liked him? Could I have loved him? We might have been a family – isn't that what everyone thought, when they passed us in the street in the months that followed? Elizabeth Rothwell, the sad beauty who was almost happy but never quite got there, blighted by fate and her strange daughter.

As I stood on the beach, I imagined her wandering the garden above in the rain, checking on the boiling fruit and planning to bake cakes for Mr Bowen. She would be storing things in jars for the winter ahead, mending a dress, sorting out her library books for return. I closed my eyes as the rain got heavier. I didn't want to watch the sea. The wind rose and I could feel the years weaving and unfolding out ahead of us. An ageing mother and daughter, arms linked, walking along a cold, grey seafront. We would not be happy, but immune to the ways of the world; we would take tea and read. This was what we were good for, and odd dreams that told of the future, though no one would believe anything that we said. Of course, she didn't get old, and we left the town to live in a flat in the city. Not everything I dreamed of came true; I was as guilty of failure as anyone else.

I opened my eyes to shouts and two men running on the beach. One of them took his jacket off and waded into the sea, a lifebuoy under his arm. There was a fishing boat far out and I wondered for a second if I was wrong and maybe Mr Bowen would be saved. The rain got heavier, I could feel it slipping down my neck, my jumper already damp, and I started to shiver.

More people came to the beach. The man who swam out after Mr Bowen could still be seen far out in the waves. Someone else held a buoy helpless in their hands and one of the fishermen was starting up the boat. I waited and watched, and I wondered would the sea give him up easily or would it take days? Like when Marcus and Lewis's dads were lost and they waited weeks for the bodies to wash up along the coast. I looked up to our house outlined against large black clouds. It was cowering, forlorn, in the strangely dark morning sky. She would be drinking coffee at the table now and reading one of the books he had lent her because she liked to hold his things in her hands. The familiar idleness would have returned, the preparations for winter put aside for a time. She was waiting for him because he had come back to her, unlike my father.

People emerged from nowhere and lined the promenade and the shoreline. We had a sense for days like these, a collective fear and then guilt descending, as if we were responsible for the sea and the people it took away. There was shouting and eyes scanned the water, willing the lifeboat to appear. It should have been rounding the cliff edges of the Ridge, where the water was deep, dark and green. I didn't know how long it took to drown, perhaps no longer than a breath. I shivered again, uncontrollably now. The damp had settled on my chest. The people around me came and went, blurred outlines running and shouting, arms raised, calls unheard, unanswered. A siren went off somewhere, far away down the coast, a beacon to warn the other towns of dangerous seas and the possibility of death.

They would hoist their red flags.

* * *

We never went back to the town. After we sold up it was as if we had never lived there at all, it was never spoken of. A professional family bought the house and played golf with our old solicitor. My mother fired him, and got a new one in the city, someone who knew nothing about us or who we had once been. She put the money from the house sale in the bank and spent a modest amount on an apartment that overlooked a gated square in the city. A glossy woman showed us around and pointed out the expensive fixtures and extolled the life of privacy we would enjoy there. We were rich in a way. Letters came that suggested various investments we might consider should we be so inclined. She would put them in the stove and watch them melt. I thought we might travel, but we did not.

We saw Mr Bowen's wife at his memorial service. It was in a cavernous, dark city church, freezing cold with flickering candles and stained-glass windows. A dull September day, the city dirty and loud, people pushing past us off the train, dust blowing in the brisk wind of the narrow, mean street. We sat close to the back of the church. A giant statue of the Virgin Mary perched on a flimsy pedestal leaned over our heads. My mother kept her sunglasses on which drew more attention to us and seemed vaguely sacrilegious, but she looked like a film star. Her lips painted a deep red, a thin string of antique pearls around her neck, and not a tear shed.

His wife was tall and thin, her back bowed with grief; caring friends sat on either side. People from the university, people who didn't know he no longer loved her and that he regretted most things about their lives. He was in love with the dark, reluctant beauty in the back row. His wife, however, looked after his legacy magnificently. One of his books, that people had forgotten about or never read in the first place, was even reissued, though she didn't publish the one he had been working on that last summer. I presumed it was because my mother had seeped into the words and it was a reminder of his betrayal.

My therapist tells me to go back; to go back to that hot summer and find myself again, to view my actions like a god high above in the clouds.

'What would you say if you met yourself on the promenade with all that you know now?' she asks.

I would let Marcus kiss me that night on the Ridge and I would tell him I loved him. I would take Lewis by the hand and bring him home from the beach and offer him lemonade in our garden. I would say to Dr Black I did not believe in blue lights and other impossible things. This did not mean they were not true, I just chose not to believe in them. I would close my eyes when they hovered high above my head. And I would stop Mr Bowen from swimming out that day and give him back to my mother.

If you imagined something differently, was that not atonement enough? You cannot change the past, but only think about it in a new way. The future offers so many more possibilities, that is why I have always preferred it. You can dream up a better version of yourself. The past is something to forget, until you can't any longer.

The waves were rising and the light was fading, the beach seeping into the sea, the sea merging with the pale sky. It was a day that struggled, that never really began. My mother would be trying to read at the table. She would switch on the lamp and feel guilty for doing so because it wasted electricity. Her dark hair over her eyes as she looked at the words in his book, not really taking them in, the secret, silent part of her waiting, waiting for him to come back and pull the strands back from her face. They had been given a second chance, all past sins were forgotten, and a new life was waiting.

If I'd had the strength to raise my head from the sand, I would have seen it, the dim light in her window. It would have guided me home on that dark, tragic morning. I imagined Mr Bowen might have seen it too, alone and far out in the wild, uncaring sea. A last glimmer of hope, like a faint breath of life, shining from our house high on the cliffs beyond. And Marcus also, working in his shop, perhaps it might have enticed him up the cliff steps and into my life again.

But it didn't bring either of them back, and I went home to my ever silent mother and a kitchen filled with the aroma of cooked apples. All the empty, sterilized jars lined up on the counter, waiting for winter. Our lives set again, bound together by all the impossible things we never dared to speak about, the strange harvest of our thoughts.

Acknowledgements

I am deeply grateful to a number of people who helped me in the writing of this book. My agent Sara O'Keeffe whose trust in my work gives me the freedom to create stories such as these. Sarah Hodgson, my editor, for her insight and understanding and also for her faith in my writing. I am ever thankful for her knowledge and support and that of the whole Corvus team.

To my family because I know it is not easy to live with someone for whom imaginary worlds are sometimes more real than anything else. I am very grateful for your patience and love.